Also by R.Z.Halleson

My Name is Mike Trumpsky

The Death Called Change

Spare Them? No Profit. Remove Them? No Loss

God's Child: The Origin of Fear

Ambiguous

GOD'S CHILD:

UNRAVELING

GOD'S CHILD:

UNRAVELING

R.Z.Halleson

A Gjerda Book

R.Z. Halleson & Associates

Evanston, Illinois

R.Z. Halleson & Associates
1 Calvin Circle , A-405
Evanston, Illinois 60201
www.halleson.com

God's Child: Unraveling/R.Z. Halleson -- 1st ed.
ISBN 978-0-9851023-1-9

If one were willing to admit that the Bible is an inspired book, then it was no use picking out of it what agreed more or less with one's own taste or opinions of probability and baking one's own religious cake of that.

—THE WILD ORCHID
by Sigrid Undset, winner of the 1928 Nobel Prize for Literature

Table of Contents

1

Taken

The bicycle speeded up as the girl approached the hill. She gave her bike a last push of speed to pedal as far up the hill as she could before the bike slowed from the climb, and she'd have to stand to use her weight to pump the pedals. In a couple of minutes she would get off the bike and walk it to the top of the rise before mounting it again for the last downhill glide of her journey home from school. Her routine was the same. She was the child at the end of the line, and had to ride alone after the other children had veered off to their own farms.

The man had been watching from his dark green pickup truck parked near the creek at the bottom of the hill. He took no chances. He had backed his truck well into the foliage to hide it, and she hadn't spotted him as she rode quickly past. Nobody had ever been with her on her ride toward home. Nobody had ever come to meet her. She was always alone on this stretch of the road. Today was the day that he'd make his move.

Overgrown weeds and vines covered the small steep cliff on the left side of the road leading up the hill, and thick bushes and small trees separated the road and the ditch from the adjacent field on the right. Nobody would see him, but he had to move quickly before she got back on her bicycle at the top of the hill to make the downward descent to her farm home.

He started the engine and pulled out onto dirt road. Fresh gravel would probably be spread on it later this summer, but for now it was dry and smooth enough for a bicycle's easy journey. Still pedaling hard up the hill, she wasn't far ahead. Hearing the truck behind her, she turned her head briefly, jumped off the bike and moved to the side of the road to let him pass.

The man pulled his truck slowly beside the girl and brought it to a stop just ahead of her. She wasn't alarmed yet, so he got out of the truck and said, "I wonder if you could help me. I need some directions." He smiled at her. "These country roads get very confusing." He walked toward her. Seeing her look of suspicion, he moved quickly, grabbed her arms, spun her around and wound cellophane tape around her wrists. This tape was easy to get at any drugstore, couldn't be traced, and held well when wrapped around at least twice while twisting it. Before she could scream, he covered her mouth with his hand. Ah, practice makes perfect, he thought. It's all in the element of surprise.

The girl began kicking at him and trying to get away, but he laughed out loud at her struggling. These farm girls were strong, and that's why they were desired. They were generally healthier than city, or even town, girls, and so they lasted longer. He would take her home and see if she was a prize heifer or if she was one of those rare little cows that he could play with for a while before delivery. The man taped the girl's mouth shut and pushed her to the ground winding tape around her ankles. While she lay in the grass at the side of the road crying and trying to roll away, the man shoved her bicycle into the ditch out of sight.

He reached into the flatbed of his truck and pushed the tarp to one side. He heaved the child onto the old mattress, pulled the tarp over her and secured it on all sides to prevent it blowing aside during the long journey back to his place. The mattress was crucial. When he'd first gotten into this business, he had thrown his first girl and a little boy on the metal floor in the back of the pickup, and by the time he'd gotten home, the kids were so brain damaged from their heads bouncing on the metal that they couldn't be sold. He'd buried them barely alive in a small patch of woods a couple of miles away from his property where he couldn't be connected to them if they were found. Since then he'd been more careful. Suppliers such as himself were expected to deliver children and teens in good condition, with the higher prices going for virgin girls. This one looked like she would be a pure one, innocent with no prior sexual experience. He'd check to be sure after he unloaded her.

He knew that there were other entrepreneurs in the child delivery business in this area, but he didn't know who they were and didn't care. Sometimes he could spot one who was watching a particular child, and if he was spotted in return, the two men might nod briefly to each other, but they never approached one another. Nobody knew his name, not even the businessmen to whom he delivered the children. No records were kept, certainly not by him, and very likely not by them. If two or more children were taken from areas close together, each child would have been snatched in isolation by individuals who were not acquainted. Suppliers who operated in cities often worked in pairs or even in groups, but in the country that wasn't necessary. It wasn't hard to find children alone if one knew where to look, and he didn't want to share his tax-free income with a partner or with anyone else, especially, thank god, his wife who had left him long ago. He smiled. What an idiot she had been to walk out on him. She could have been living in luxury now with the money he was making. He already had more than he knew what to do with. Someday he'd quit this work and move south to a warmer climate, maybe find another wife and, who knows, have kids of his own.

It was dark when he pulled into his driveway in the hills outside of Baraboo, Wisconsin. The dogs had begun barking the minute he turned into his private road. Ah, somebody was glad to see him. He jumped out of the truck, petted the dogs dancing around him, and walked to the back of the pickup. Untying the ropes holding down the tarp, he said, "Hey fellas. I got a new one for you. You've been lonely since the last batch left, I know. Poor boys," he crooned as he pulled the girl off the mattress, hoisted her over his shoulder, and let the dogs sniff her before he carried her toward the house.

Pushing open the unlocked kitchen door, he walked directly across the room and down the stairs into the basement pulling the string hanging from the ceiling to turn on the single light bulb illuminating the room. One light was enough. The concrete cellar wasn't large, but it was big enough to hold eight or ten children before he shipped them out. A stack of thin mattresses was piled in the corner. A hand-built wooden table sat directly under the light for examination purposes. The only other door visible in this basement room opened outside to stone steps leading up to the pen and an outhouse. With four big dogs ready to attack if they tried to climb over the high wooden fence, the kids, even the boys, were too traumatized to attempt escape. Anyway, they had no idea what was in store for them, so why should they be afraid? He was generally kind to them during the weeks and sometimes months that they were here, even providing extra blankets on cold nights, so that most of the girls and boys cooperated when he told them to do tasks for him such as cleaning the house and the basement or washing the clothes. If they yelled when playing out in the cattle pen, who was to hear them? The only sounds that the children would hear were himself, each other, the dogs, birds singing in the trees, and the occasional hum of the generator that provided electricity. It was peaceful. He had developed the perfect setup, and he was proud of his accomplishment. Furthermore, he enjoyed his work. It suited him.

The man put the girl on the wooden table, pulled off her shoes, tossed them to the floor, and began running his hands over her body. Yes, nice. Her breasts were budding; she was suitably plump. He pulled on a rubber glove, cut the tape to free her legs, moistened his middle finger in his mouth and pushed it inside her. "Good girl," he said. "You're a good one!"

He pulled the tape from her mouth and cut her hands free. She tried to roll off the table away from him, but he caught her and lifted her gently to the floor. "Now, here are the rules," he said. She shrank away from him, but he ignored it; she'd come around after a few days.

"You will pull one mattress from the pile to sleep on. There are blankets in the box in the corner. You may use as many as you need for now, but you'll have to share them when the others come. There is a sink in here, and a toilet outside. Do not climb on the fence. The dogs don't like it. They will tear you apart and kill you if you get to the other side. For now, I will bring you one meal each day; later there may be more if anyone needs to put on weight. Behave, and no harm will come to you while you are here." He turned and went up the stairs, closing the door to the kitchen and pushing the bolt to lock her in.

Sometimes the man took a couple of days to work around the house and yard, but right now he was in a hurry to gather as many children as he could and haul the next batch in his van to the LaCrosse warehouse before the middle of July. Once there, each would be examined and confined to an individual crate before being loaded with the goods of other suppliers onto palettes and subsequently into the back of a big nondescript truck for transport to Chicago. As far as he knew, the children were primed somewhere in Chicago where they would be taught about what the clients wanted from them, but he thought that some might be sold locally also. Pregnant teens might be kept until their babies were born to be sold to lawyers who would find adoptive parents willing to pay a high price; then the mothers would be sent onward to their new careers. He smiled. Where they went from there was anybody's guess. He didn't care as long as he got a good price for his own batch. He was known as a supplier who consistently brought in quality goods. He had long ago become a professional.

The girl stood with her back glued against the cold concrete wall for several minutes staring up at the door that had just closed and locked her in. She was so tired. Exhausted. She had dozed some on the mattress in the truck, but it had hurt to lay bound in that uncomfortable position, and she kept waking up stunned, in a state of terror such as she had never known before. This wasn't real. This wasn't happening. In a few minutes she would wake up at home in her own room. She closed her eyes and opened them again. No. The table where the man had touched her was still there. She could still feel the sensation of his finger pushing deep inside her, and felt dirty, violated in a place that, before now, she had barely known existed. The crude steep staircase sat silently, empty. She heard a dog yelp once outside.

She felt faint, but caught herself before falling. *I need to sleep. When I wake up in the morning, I'll smell bacon, and Mom will call me. That's what will happen. I know it. Just sleep now. The sooner I go to sleep, the sooner I will be home again.*

She limped to the stack of thin mattresses and pulled one to the floor. She went to the box of blankets and retrieved the top one from the box. Shaking possible bugs from it, she clutched it around her as she collapsed onto the makeshift bed and huddled beneath the cover trying to hide from the light. *I can't turn it off. I can't turn it off. It will be dark if I turn it off. Sobbing, she finally fell into a deep troubled sleep.*

The girl was awakened to daylight streaming in the high windows and by footsteps lumbering down the rickety stairs. Startled, she opened her eyes, but did not move.

"Wake up," said the man. "I brought a box of food down for you. I'll be gone for a few days so you'll have to make it last. Since you're the only one here yet, you won't run out. There are some plates and bowls and forks and spoons in the cupboard over there. There's a can opener too, but you'll have to eat everything cold. I can't let you upstairs to cook until I come back. Oh, and there's a radio on the counter. I put in new batteries after the last bunch left, so you can have some music if you want it."

He set the cardboard box on the wooden table, and turning to go up the stairs, said, "Don't worry about the dogs. I'll feed them before I leave. They won't bother you if you stay off the fence. You can go outside as much as you want. We started a little garden out back, but the vegetables are just starting to sprout. You won't be able to eat any of them for a few weeks."

Weeks? Weeks? The girl sat up and stared at him but said nothing. *What did he mean? I can't be here for weeks! I have to go home. I have to go to school. She began to cry, but he ignored her.*

"I'll see you in about four or five days. Be a good girl."

The girl heard the man moving around on the floor above her. Then he went outside talking to the dogs as they followed him away from the house. The engine of his pickup truck started up, and she heard it moving down the drive as the dogs ran after it barking.

2

Unraveling

Silje awakened from her dozing as she felt the car lift itself up over the railroad tracks and then slant downward into the curving driveway. Pa turned the car around, backed it up a few feet, and pulled forward to a stop in front of the garage door. “It’s not going to rain tonight. I’m going to leave it out,’ he said. Ma mumbled her assent as she opened the passenger-side car door. They were all tired.

Too many relatives. Too much noise. Too much cake. Yuk! I’m glad I went to the bathroom at Aunt Lilah’s. I won’t have to get the flashlight and go outside to the toilet here . . . spiders. Silje got out of the old four-door green Packard and trudged over the gravel driveway and onto the grass leading to the short sidewalk. She heard her parents walking behind her. She felt as if she were barely awake. I want to crawl into bed.

The full moon lit the path as Silje put one foot in front of the other. Suddenly she was wide awake. She was hearing footsteps behind her. They were going to kill her. She knew it. At any moment the knife would enter her back, slice through her body and come out in front. Terror threatened to overwhelm her as she quickened her own steps. Could she get away? Could she run into the house and get into her bedroom and shut the door? She forced herself to continue walking as if nothing was going to happen. *It's Ma and Pa. They are not going to hurt me.* Silje mind-talked to herself silently trying to calm the almost overwhelming fear that had come suddenly out of nowhere. *The footsteps belong to my parents. They won't touch me.* She knew that she could turn around and look back at her mother and father to confirm that they were not running toward her and that neither one was holding a knife, but she continued walking looking straight ahead. *They won't. They will not hurt me. They will not hurt me!* At any moment now, she would reach the porch and climb the steps. She would cross the small porch, open the screen door, and push open the unlocked wooden door containing a window large enough to see who might be standing on the porch if a stranger came. By the time her mother entered the kitchen to light the kerosine lamp on the table, Silje would be in her room, in her pajamas, and under the covers. *No one will know what's in my head. It's a trick that my mind is playing. It's not real.*

Ever since Silje had moved with her parents to this farm, it seemed that there was nothing fun to do. The farm was small compared to the farm next to it where they had previously lived together with her uncle's family. She didn't know exactly why they had moved, but her father and his brother had been arguing more this past year, so when the old couple on this farm died, Silje's parents Alex and Pauline Reiersen decided to buy it. There had been no heirs claiming the farm and they had gotten a good price through the county court for it. They had moved in June, right after school ended. Silje was twelve and would be going into eighth grade in the fall.

The farm was not in good shape. Every day her father was outside picking rocks from neglected fields so that he could plant some late crops to support the cattle that he was accumulating. Her mother was busy pulling weeds and tilling the garden, rescuing existing vegetables, asparagus, rhubarb, and ground cherries, and hoping that her new plantings would yield enough vegetables for canning to get them through the winter. Silje helped her mother wash clothes by hand in cold water in the cellar underneath the living room: whites first, then colored, all using the same soapy water and the same rinse water. She turned the handle on the ringer to crank the clothes one by one through the two rubber rollers to squeeze the water out, and then carried them outside to hang them on the line. When they were dry, she would gather them in a basket and bring them inside to iron them with an iron that was heated on top of the cook stove in the kitchen. It was work! Ugh. But at least it was something to do.

How the old couple had gotten through the winters was puzzling. The house was a one-room log cabin to which three rooms had been added on. The first add-on was an elongated kitchen two steps down from the room with logs across its ceiling; the kitchen floor had settled into a slight downward slant so that anything round that dropped on the floor rolled to one side. Next to the kitchen was a small bedroom in which Alex and Pauline slept. Silje's bedroom was in the far corner three steps up from her parent's room and two small steps down into the original log room used as a living room. There were doors to close off the bedrooms, but none between the living room and the two very steep steps down into the kitchen.

The house stayed reasonably cool if they did all their cooking out in the summer kitchen, a separate one-room shed next to the house, but Alex would have to insulate the main house before winter and add a small furnace in the living room if they were to be comfortable living in this house year-round.

Most of the apple trees in the orchard next to the house were crab apple trees yielding wormy fruit too sour to eat but great for making pies, applesauce, and jam. One of these trees was perfect for climbing and sitting comfortably in the branches. It became a favorite place for Silje to rest and daydream and make up stories of what she would do if she were rich and famous like the characters in the library books her mother read. Alex put up a swing on another tree and when Robbie, Silje's seven-year-old cousin from the previous farm, came to play, they would take turns in the swing telling stories to each other.

One afternoon Silje's father came into the house to find her. "Come with me," said Alex. "You have to drive the tractor. It takes too long for me to keep getting on and off every time I need to move the wagon just a few feet."

I don't know how to drive the tractor. I've never even been on the tractor.

Alex went back outside before Silje had time to answer him. She followed.

Her father walked quickly back to the field beyond the pond where he had been working preparing the soil to plant a late crop of corn. More rocks needed to be removed before the field could be plowed. Silje ran to keep up with him. When they arrived, Alex got on the tractor, started the engine, and said, "When I yell 'drive', then you drive a few feet forward until I shout 'stop'."

He got off and walked back to the wagon and began to pick up softball-sized rocks from the ground to toss into the flatbed wagon ignoring her. Silje had no idea what to do. She climbed up to the seat of the tractor and looked around. She tried turning the steering wheel slightly and saw that the small wide-apart front tires responded. She had seen her father push down on a lever near the floor on the right side. *Maybe that's how to get it to move.*

"Drive!" Alex yelled.

Trying not to panic, Silje leaned forward and pushed her right foot down on the lever near the floor. Slowly the tractor responded and rolled forward on the downward incline pulling the wagon along with it.

"Stop!" shouted her father.

Silje lifted her foot off the lever and the tractor crept to a stop. *Okay. So far. So good.* After a few more "drives" and "stops," Silje realized that there had to be more to driving the tractor than this. If it were pointed uphill, the tractor might roll backward when she put her foot on this lever. It wasn't like the tractor was really moving because she was making it move. It was just passively rolling downhill when she pushed this one lever. There must be a brake somewhere. *I don't dare ask Pa what to do. He's too mad right now, and he'll yell at me. I'd better figure this out myself.* She gently pushed down the similar floor lever on the opposite side. Nothing. *There's gotta be a reason why it's there.*

"Drive!"

Silje pushed down the right floor lever and let the tractor roll until she heard "Stop!" Without thinking she stood on both the right and left levers at the same time and the tractor jerked to a sudden stop. *That's gotta be the brake! I found it.* When the tractor got to the end of the field, her father called it quits. It was time to do the milking. Silje got down from the tractor, watched her father climb onto the tractor seat, step on the right floor lever, push the upright stick in the middle of the tractor floor to another position, and move his foot to a raised button near the right lever. The tractor roared away down the lane. *So that's how it's done. If he makes me help tomorrow, I'll try that. Maybe he'll think that I knew it all along.*

Silje walked slowly back to the house. There were almost three more months before school started again. *What will I do until then? If Ma gets another box of books from the Madison library, that will keep me busy for a while. I can read mine in a couple of days and then I'll read hers. We can't read at the table anymore because Pa doesn't like it, but I can read in my bedroom, or in the apple tree, or in the living room if nobody is sitting in there.*

The house was empty when she got back. Pauline was in the barn helping Alex. Now that there were just two adults on the farm, Ma had to help Pa with outside chores as well as doing household work. Only a month ago, Silje had been a part of a household with four adults plus a hired man, a hired girl and two cousins. She had never experienced loneliness before, and hadn't yet put a name to this feeling of emptiness and boredom without other people constantly around. Not that she had liked having so many people underfoot. Mostly she had stayed out of the adults' way and avoided them as much as she could. Her older cousin Nils rarely paid any attention to her, but Robbie, five years younger, followed her around wanting to play. She missed having him around.

She had fed the chickens and picked eggs earlier so there was nothing left for her to do. Silje went into her bedroom and flopped down on the bed. She saw her pad of paper on the dresser, retrieved it along with a pencil, and sat down on the bed to draw. She was still engrossed in her experimental drawings of faces, when she heard her parents come into the kitchen.

"We're not in the Homestead school district anymore, so Silje will have to go to Clockmaker School,"

What??? Silje looked up, alarmed.

"That will be a problem because Clockmaker is way down the in valley. I don't know how she'll get to school and home again. We'll have to drive her both ways. There aren't any other children up here on the highway."

"She'll have to take her bicycle," said Alex.

"It's too far, and the hills are too steep. We can't drive her both ways every day. We'll be too busy. We could drive her in the morning, and have her walk home in the afternoon."

"That would work in the summer, but winter will be a problem, even if we could get through. The county doesn't plow the side roads right away. There are too many of them. The highways get plowed first."

Silje walked from her bedroom and stood at the top of the steps going down from the living room to the kitchen. "I am NOT going to Clockmaker School," she announced. "I'm going back to Homestead next year!" She spun around and marched back into her bedroom. Shocked at herself for talking so boldly to her parents, Silje sat on the side of her bed waiting for the response that was sure to come, her heart thumping. She remembered the time when her mother had chased her through the house slapping a wet dish rag at her for talking back. It was funny even at the time, but she hadn't dared to laugh, at least not until her mother stopped chasing her and went back to washing dishes. Silence. Nobody in the kitchen spoke further.

This was more serious. *No way. There is no way I'm going to Clockmaker School. I don't even know where it is. There are probably all of two children who go there with a teacher who has never read a book in her life. I am not going there. Not.*

"Come and eat," called Pauline.

Silje walked into the kitchen. Alex was seated at the table and Pauline was filling his bowl with the hot steaming chicken stew left from last night's supper. He sprinkled salt and pepper generously onto the stew and stirred it with his spoon. Silje slid onto the wooden chair and reached for a slice of homemade bread. She preferred the white Wonder Bread from the store, but that was a special treat purchased only to make sandwiches when they knew that relatives would be coming to visit.

No one spoke. Silje had made her stand, and would say no more about it. She was going back to Homestead School. *Period!*

Just after noon dinner the next day, Silje put on a clean shirt and fresh socks. Her jeans weren't especially dirty so they would do. Slipping her feet into her old penny-loafers, she put her wrapped present into a paper bag so that it wouldn't get damaged if she suddenly dropped it. "I'm going now, Ma," she said.

"Okay. Be home by five. We need you to help in the barn tonight."

Hopefully I'll be home long before that. I don't even want to go to Clara's birthday party. I can't stand her. Just because we were in the same grade last year doesn't mean I have to be her friend, but that's exactly what everyone else seems to expect. Ugh. Truly ugh!

Silje pulled her bicycle out of the garage and put the wrapped box containing a 500-word puzzle into the basket that was wired to the front handlebars. She wheeled the bike up the newly graveled driveway until she got to the railroad tracks. Crossing the tracks, she got on the bike, coasted the few yards down the short incline to Highway 27 and turned north.

The Mitbys had been renting their farm for just over a year and never really seemed to get settled. Clara's father Delling didn't seem very energetic and her mother Selma did most of the work around the place or so Silje had heard her mother say. Clara's chubby younger brother Paul worked alongside his mother and never said much. Silje didn't like him either.

Maybe there will be other kids from Homestead School at the party. In the grade ahead of Silje and Clara had been several girls, some of who lived nearby. *Maybe they were in-*

vited even though they've graduated. They won't start high school until September. Maybe they still care about Homestead kids. If even one of them comes, it will save my life. If I'm the only one there, it will be torture. How will I get outta there? Clara is a bossy cow.

Silje pedaled quickly past the tall evergreens shading and concealing the Hoffman's farmhouse and turned her bike into the Mitby's driveway on the left of the highway. Their farm buildings were set way back from the road. The drive curved slightly and was long enough to look like a side road, but the Mitbys was the only farm to which it led. The house was extraordinarily large for a farm house. An old woman, the owner of the farm, lived in one half of the divided house, but Silje had never seen her. *Creepy. How can Clara sleep at night? It must be like having a ghost in the house if the old lady walks up and down the stairway at night even though she has her own stairwell on her side of the house.*

As she parked her bicycle next to the front porch, Silje heard children's voices in the backyard. She walked around the side of the house and spotted Clara. "Here, I brought you a present," said Silje. "Happy Birthday."

"Thanks," said Clara. "You're kind of late. We've already started the games."

"That's okay. I'll just watch until they start another one." Silje sat down under a tree and began blowing through flat blades of grass held tightly between her thumbs making a loud buzzing vibration.

"Hey, how do you do that?" One of last year's fourth-graders ran up to her. Soon Silje was surrounded by younger children practicing blade-blowing. *Maybe this party won't be so bad after all.*

"We're going to play hide and seek until it's time for sandwiches and cake," ordered Clara walking up to Silje and the children gathered around her. "I'll be the first 'It.' One - two - three." . . . She began counting even as she walked toward a nearby tree, leaned against it covering her eyes. The children ran away from Silje and scrambled to find hiding places among the trees and bushes around the house. Silje looked around. *Hmm. Where's the best place? Nobody said we couldn't go inside."* Silje walked around to the front of the house, past a child hiding behind a railing on the porch, opened the screen door and stepped inside. She could smell the odor of freshly baked cookies and cake as she walked into the kitchen.

"Can I help set out the plates?" she asked Clara's mother.

"Isn't everyone outside playing a game?" asked Selma Mitby, her dark stringy hair looking like it hadn't been washed yet this week.

"Yes, the little kids are, but I thought I might help in here instead. The cookies smelled so good."

Selma laughed at her. "Oh, all right. Help yourself, and then you can fill the glasses with lemonade."

She's making fun of me, just like she always does. She thinks I came in here just for the cookies. Silje turned away, her mouth tightly shut. *I'll show her. I won't take any cookies. I won't eat even one the whole time I'm here.* Feeling put down, Silje poured lemonade into the glasses and took them out to the small table out on the porch. She was sorry that she had gone into the house, but it was too late to escape her offer of help so she carried sandwiches and other snacks out to the porch until the task was finished.

"You can call the children to come and pick up their plates of food," said Selma. "I think Clara is still in the backyard."

Silje walked around to the backyard and found Clara hiding by the side of the outhouse. "Your mom says to tell the kids to come and get their plates. Want me to help find them all?"

"Mm mm, Let's just tell Margaret. She's 'It' right now. She can find them. Let's run and be first in line."

You'd be first in line anyway since you're the birthday girl, but I'll go with you. Won't hurt.

Maybe I can get one of the cookies that I'm not going to eat. Silje had already changed her mind about the cookies. She followed behind Clara. None of the older girls from Homestead had come to the party, so she was the only one of Clara's age. Everyone else was younger. The Mitbys had no family in Vernon County with cousins that might have come. *Maybe they don't have any aunts and uncles at all. Maybe they just appeared out of nowhere. Maybe everybody hated Clara so much that the whole family was chased out of their former county. Wouldn't be surprised.*

Clara and Silje sat with their plates of food on the front porch steps. Other children walked past them and sat on the lawn. Clara ate quickly. "I'm finished, Ma. We can cut the cake and open the presents now."

Selma brought out a large cake and lit twelve candles. "Okay everybody. Let's sing Happy Birthday. Then we can all have birthday cake." Clara rose suddenly and started up the porch steps, knocking over Silje's glass of lemonade still half full as she passed.

"Ohhh. My jeans got wet!" lamented Silje.

"You put your glass where it could get kicked," laughed Clara, not stopping. "What did you expect? Don't worry. Your pants will dry." As Clara blew out the candles on her cake, the children sang the birthday song and brought their plates up the porch steps to receive pieces of white cake with chocolate frosting.

Silje walked down the steps through the children and tried to blot the big wet spot on her jeans with some weeds. It wasn't working. *I don't care. This is a stupid party. I didn't want to be here anyway.*

Clara was opening her gifts while surrounded by younger children eating their cake up on the porch and exclaiming over Clara's presents as she ripped off the paper. Nobody was looking in Silje's direction. She slipped around the side of the house, got her bicycle, and walked it to the edge of the yard. Without looking back to see if she was noticed, Silje mounted her bike and pedaled as fast as she could up the road to the highway.

I'll never go to another one of Clara's parties. I'll never agree to go along even if our mothers want us to get together. Never. I hate her. She's stupid. If I am ever forced to be in the same room with her, I- I-I'll kill her. I'll make her disappear. I'll figure out a way. I will. She'd better look out. Make HER go to stupid Clockmaker School next year.

3

Absorbing Pollyanna

The summer dragged on. Silje took any excuse to help out in the fields with her father to escape being cooped up inside doing dishes or *ugh* cleaning the house or ironing clothes. She had an aunt who actually ironed the sheets for the beds! It was her prissy aunt Joella who used to be her Sunday School teacher. *She probably irons underwear too!*

Silje enjoyed driving the tractor now that she'd figured out the relationship between brake, accelerator, and clutch. She could switch gears with ease not killing the engine. Pa had finally explained some of it to her, so she didn't have to sound ignorant when her older cousin Nils compared tractors with her.

The men from the REA had come today to work on hooking up the electricity, and Silje stayed out of their way. She couldn't imagine what it would be like to have real lights in the house instead of the kerosene lamp, so she decided not to think about it. When it happened, it would happen.

Silje was bored. There was nothing to do. It was late afternoon, but the sun would be up for hours yet, and her parents were busy somewhere paying no attention to her. "Come on Pal. Let's go down in the woods." The half-grown Collie-ish mutt followed her whenever she was outside. Pa had gotten him several weeks ago from another farmer who'd had too many left from last year's litter. He was going to be a natural in herding the cows, the man had told Pa. Silje was growing to love this long-haired black, brown, and white dog.

The two walked past the barn and into the grassy lane where the tractor could access the fields on this side of the farm. The fields were on the left of the lane and on the right was the fenced-in pasture holding the herd of twenty-three cows and two horses. They were all further down the pasture out of sight, and Silje saw only the bull chained to a stake. The big Guernsey bull watched her as she walked past and turned his head to follow her with his eyes. The dog paid no attention, but Silje made herself walk calmly past the bull pretending that she didn't see him although she kept an eye on him in case he tried to break loose from his chain and come after her. If he made any move at all, she would turn around and run as fast as she could back to the house. There was no question in Silje's mind that the monster bull could break through the barbed wire fence with ease. Bulls could be very nasty creatures as many farmers had found out when they lost control of an angry bull.

Pal ran ahead of Silje, jumped into the gully just before the woods, found a path up the other side, and disappeared among the trees.

Silje descended backwards down the side of the gully choosing her steps carefully while hanging onto rocks and roots sticking out of the gully's wall. There were only a few puddles here and there left from the rainstorm a few days ago. Pa was planning to rent some earthmoving equipment sometime this summer to fill in the gully and level the land for use as a field. Their farm was only eighty acres, and he wanted every bit of it to be productive. Stepping around the puddles and trying to avoid the mud, Silje followed the path that Pal had taken and ascended the other side to enter the woods. Pal was nowhere in sight.

It was more fun to play in the woods when her cousins were with her. They'd use sticks, branches, and leaves to create outlines of pretend houses or castles or cowboy-ranches and become exciting characters in their dramas which could go on days if they were able to come back and if rain didn't wash their creations away.

Today, she was alone.

The day was hot, but in the shade under the trees Silje didn't think about it. The bushes and other foliage were not so thick that she couldn't push her way through easily. There was no breeze. Once she heard the dog yelp close by, but she didn't see him. He was around somewhere; that's all she needed to know.

Coming into a clearing, Silje thought *This would be a good place to play. Maybe I can set up the village where Pollyanna lives, and I will be her.* Silje was known throughout this large extended Norwegian-American family as the girl who read books, and one Christmas she had received twelve new books as gifts from various relatives. It was heaven. Of course she had read them all in just a few weeks and then read them over and over again: The Bobbsey Twins, Cherry Ames Army Nurse, and Nancy Drew Mysteries. She borrowed her cousin Nils's Tarzan books too and read them all.

Currently she was reading the Pollyanna series about an eleven-year-old girl who went to live with a grumpy aunt when her missionary parents died. Pollyanna had learned from her father to always look on the bright side and find something to be glad about no matter how bad things seemed. What Silje didn't realize was how thoroughly she was beginning to absorb Pollyanna's philosophy as she read the series again and again. When something bad happened, Silje practiced looking for something positive that could come out of the bad. When she thought mean thoughts, she practiced flipping those thoughts upside down into good thoughts. It was hardest when she thought about Clara who seemed to ridicule Silje whenever they were together.

Maybe Clara is an exception. Everything needs an exception, right? Clara is the exception to the Pollyanna rule. I can hate her all I want as long as I don't tell anyone how I feel.

Silje walked across the grass and bare dirt through dry leaves toward the large tree in the center, when suddenly what had seemed to be just another dried mud patch gave way under her foot and she suddenly sank up to her knee. As she felt her leg being sucked into the mud hole, she threw herself forward flat on the ground beyond the mud patch to prevent her other leg from slipping into the hole. She twisted onto her back, sat up, pulled her leg squishing out of the watery mud and pushed herself on her buttocks away from the hole, which settled back into the seemingly benign patch of dirt that it had been before it showed itself to be alive. She stared at the hole, stunned by what she had just experienced.

This isn't mud at all. It's water that looks like mud. If I would have stepped into it with both feet, I would have sunk all the way down and nobody would ever have found me. I would have disappeared. Would anyone have noticed? Would anybody care? What if nobody even cared?

Silje used leaves to wipe off the watery mud from her leg and foot. She took off her shoe and sock, wiped the outside of the shoe and put it back on without the sock. *It's a good thing that I stepped on it with only one foot. And maybe it's a good thing that it happened at all, because now I can avoid these patches of dirt just in case there are bigger ones that are even more dangerous.*

Still shaken, Silje tucked her wet sock into a jeans pocket and began to stand up, but something would not allow it. Heavy pressure was pushing down on both shoulders forcing her to stay in place. Silje froze. She couldn't move. The pressure wasn't painful, but it was strong and it was heavy. It was like huge hands holding her down. Her mind raced. What was it? Who was nearby? She hadn't seen anyone in the woods. She hadn't heard anyone approach, and surely she would have heard someone walking through the leaves and brush. There was no one here. What was it? What was holding her down? Silje tensed, waited helplessly, and after a few seconds that seemed like forever, the pressure lifted as suddenly as it had descended upon her.

Silje stood up. She looked all around, and saw nothing but the silent woods surrounding the clearing. No squirrels. No birds singing. No flies or bees. Silence. She felt a presence as if something or someone was there, but it couldn't be. There was nothing in sight except trees, bushes, dead leaves on the ground, and tall weeds. It wasn't possible. She felt cold. Hesitating, then with growing terror, she began to run. She ran blindly through weeds, pushed past bushes scratching her arms and around trees, away from the clearing, through the woods. She slid down into the gully, and by the time she had climbed out on the other side, the dog was beside her. Together they ran up the lane and back to the house. Silje walked quickly through the kitchen past her mother and into her room. She sat down on the bed and stared at the floor. She heard the sounds of her mother moving around in the kitchen, but she wasn't comforted.

Something is wrong. Something is WRONG. There was no way that I could have known that the patch of ordinary dirt was a mud hole. It looked just like every other grassless area in the clearing. How did it get there? What was it? We've never seen anything like that before when we played in the woods. Thank you God for saving me. Thank you. I could be dead now. I could have disappeared. I can't think about the hands pushing me down. I felt them as if they were real. They were real, but nobody was there. What does this mean? Who was there with me? Nobody. But somebody!

Silje stayed in her room until her father came in for supper. "We'll wait until dark," she heard him say. "Then Silje can try it out."

Try what out? Silje walked into the kitchen and helped her mother set the table. Pot roast and dumplings tonight. Young peas fresh from the garden. Yesterday's homemade bread. Crab apple sauce with whipped cream for dessert. They ate silently, each buried in their own thoughts. The room was growing dim as the sun set to the west. The kitchen had windows only on the east side and out to the porch on the south side of the tiny house.

Pa rose from his chair and went to sit in the rocker in the front room. Ma got up, scraped leftover food from the plates into a bowl and said, "Here, take this out to the slop pail."

Silje walked out through the porch and down the steps carefully checking around the large pail at the side of the porch to be sure that there were no snakes nearby. Twice this summer, her mother had come out and seen rattlesnakes drinking from the slop pail. Snakes were more likely to come near the house when there hadn't been any rain for weeks and had nowhere else to go for water. There had been rain a few days ago, so no rattlers should be visiting. The only snakes usually this close to people were the garter snakes that lived in the vegetable garden and in the orchard.

She took the bowl back into the kitchen and handed it to her mother who was washing dishes in the sink. "Here, wipe," said Ma, pointing to a dish towel. The room was growing dark.

"We should light the lamp," said Silje picking up a wet cup.

Pa came in from the front room. "We need some light in here," he said. "Silje, go and push that button up." He pointed to a newly installed square metal plate on the wall near the door.

Silje looked at him and then at the wall. She walked to the metal plate and said, "Which one?"

"First, the one on the right," said Pa.

Silje flicked the button upward, and the kitchen was bathed in light from a glass fixture on the ceiling. "Ohhhh!"

"Turn that one off for a minute and try the other button," said Pa.

Silje did as she was told. All three of them went to the window and saw a light high on a pole half way between the house and the barn illuminating the entire farmyard.

"No more kerosene lanterns," said Pa. "We've got lights in the house, the barn, and in the yard! The REA brought us electricity, and all we need to do now is hook it up wherever we want it. I'll get an electrician out here to do the job as soon as Ma and I figure out where we need it."

Silje went to the button on the wall and flicked the kitchen light on. Then all three of them went outside into the falling darkness that no longer needed to feel so black. It was a miracle. They stood for a while admiring the farmyard at night with the light and its shadows that seemed so beautiful. The dog ran about, and finally came to sit beside them.

"I want electric lights in my room too." said Silje.

"Why not?" answered Pa. "We'll put them in all the rooms, the summer kitchen, the barn, and some of the sheds outside too. It will make everything so much easier."

4

The Worst Year of Her Life

Silje had to rely on *ugh* Clara to show her around the new school to which her parents had decided to send her. Her mother, ultra-efficient as usual, had researched all known facts, presented them to her father, and together they had decided to pay the tuition to send Silje to the elementary school for town kids in Westby. Clockmaker School, because of its location wasn't feasible as there was no way to get her to and from the one-room country school way down in the valley each day. There was too much farm work to do, plus a girl in the Clockmaker district had disappeared on her way home from school last spring and had not yet been found. The girl's bicycle was spotted in a ditch near her home when the searchers were out looking for her. Silje heard her mother and Aunt Minnie talking about it saying that Sheriff Joe Iverson was sure that she had been taken. There were no clues as to what had happened to her. That had been the deciding factor in her parents' decision to send Silje to school in town. They also thought that it would be better for her to become acquainted with more children so that she would have friends when she started high school the following year. So Silje found herself facing what she would later look back upon as the worst year of her life.

Fat ugly Clara chattered on and on as she guided Silje up two flights of stairs to the combined seventh- and eighth-grade room. Clara's family had not made enough money on the rented farm near the Reiersens and had moved to a small house on the outskirts of town which made Clara and her brother Paul eligible for town school without paying tuition.

"We came to look at the school last week, so I'd know where to go," said Clara. When they finally reached the top floor, Silje saw children milling about waiting for class to begin. Everyone seemed to know one another, and Silje felt strange and awkward. Clara marched up to a pale balding chubby man at the front of the room. "We're new," she said. "My name is Clara Mitby, and this is Silje Reiersen."

The man looked through a sheaf of papers in his hand. "Yes, you are both enrolled. Clara, you may take a seat in the fourth row second from the back. Silje, I want you in the first row of eighth graders, third seat from the front. There are two rows of seventh graders next to you. Put your lunch pails on the shelf in the classroom next to this one, and I will be calling the classes to order as soon as you get back." He turned away to speak to a skinny woman with gray frizzy hair.

Clara led Silje into a dim room filled with chairs and tables facing blackboards at the front. There were empty hooks along two sides and shelves above. A few jackets were hung on the hooks but it was still too warm outside for the heavy winter coats that would come later. The shelves above were filled with metal lunch pails. Silje and Clara pushed some lunch buckets closer together, put theirs in between, and hurried back into the main room just as Mr. Butter was ordering students to take their places.

"Eighth graders, we have two new students in the class this year. Please stand, Clara and Silje." Silje stood up and looked across to be sure Clara was also standing. She sat down quickly, embarrassed at all the people staring at her.

"Seventh graders, you are new to this classroom. Welcome. I am Mr. Butter, your head teacher, and this is Miss Cline my assistant who does most of your instruction. You will keep your school supplies in your assigned desks and take only what you need when you are called to the other classroom for specific instruction." Mr. Butter droned on explaining his expectations of what the students should and should not do. He seemed to assume that all the eighth graders knew everything already since most had been in this room last year. It was too much to keep track of; Silje's mind began to wander.

Ma drove me to Westby this morning, and she'll pick me up after school. After today, I have to ride my bike unless the weather is bad. That should work all right. It's highway all the way, flat, no hills. Thank you God for not making me go to Clockmaker. Ma said that eighth grade at the town school would prepare me for high school next year and I'd get to know other kids, so that's a good thing since I would have been the only person in my grade at Homestead, although that would have been wonderful without Clara. Who knows how many kids are at Clockmaker this year. I might have been the only kid in the whole school since that girl disappeared. All the other kids would have been smart enough to stay home and never go back! I'll bet that even the teacher is shaking in her boots, especially since she's probably all alone teaching in a school with no pupils! I've been saved. Thank you. Thank you, God!

Mr. Butter finally finished his verbal meandering by announcing that Miss Cline would be giving the seventh graders their assignments here in the home room while the eighth graders would proceed immediately into the classroom for initial math instruction and reading assignments. "Bring pencil and paper," he said.

Silje lifted the lid on her desk to retrieve the tablet and one of the pencils that Ma had purchased for her a few days ago. Her old oilcloth book bag sat on the floor at her feet containing a few other supplies that she might need. She wouldn't put them in her desk until she saw whether or not she should leave them here at the school or take them back home with her again.

The students shuffled without enthusiasm into the classroom with Silje in their midst. No one paid any attention to her. A few were poking each other and whispering, but soon settled down at the tables and chairs facing the blackboard. Silje found herself between a girl on her left and a boy on her right. "You will all continue to sit in the chairs in which you currently find yourselves for all classes for the rest of the year," said Mr. Butter. A mild groan went up from a few boys, and Mr. Butter cast his eye over the group of students. "If there is any trouble, you will find yourself in a worse position than you are now," he threatened, glaring at one of the boys. He held the boy's eye for a second longer than was probably needed, giving Silje the impression that Mr. Butter knew this boy, Edwin, very well. Edwin, slouching down in his chair, was a stocky boy with large brownish eyes and a heavy rounded jaw.

After Mr. Butter had handed out well-worn reading books and made the assignment for what was to be finished by tomorrow, he walked among the tables and handed out single sheets of printed paper one to each student. "This is a test to see how much you remember of your math instruction from last year. Put your name on the top, and work the problems. You will have forty-five minutes to finish."

Silje glanced over the paper and felt a lump gathering in her throat. She had no idea what these problems meant or how to solve them. Is this what she was supposed to have learned in her seventh grade at Homestead? Her teacher Mrs. Lunde had been so busy working with the six Homestead eighth graders preparing them for high school that, thinking she had the following year to prepare Silje and Clara with the math skills that they would need, she had let the girls' instruction slide. It had seemed as if it would be easy to get them caught up. By the time Mrs. Lunde discovered that neither of the girls would be at Homestead the next year, it was too late.

There were four story problems on the page and the rest were numerical problems. Silje tackled the numbers first. She looked over at the other students, and saw that all of them were laboring to finish the test; a few were looking up deep in thought. She knew that she was getting the answers all wrong, but she tried anyway. The story problems were impossible. There was no hope, so she scribbled a few words for each that might, by some miracle, relate to the right answer. She wondered how Clara was doing, but there was no way that she would later ask. *Let smart-aleck Clara think that she was the only dumb one!*

"When you finish, you may go back to the home room and begin your reading until everyone is done," said Mr. Butter. "Our next subject will be American History and will be held in the home room while the seventh graders use this room." Silje waited until only a couple of students were in the classroom finishing their test and tried to walk unobtrusively to the front along with them to hand in her paper.

On Thursdays, the Catholic pupils were released from class for an hour right after lunch to attend religious instruction in the basement of a nearby Lutheran church, and with written permission from parents, non-Catholic students could attend also. Only a few girls remained in the classroom on those days including Silje and Clara. They were allowed to sit together, work on homework, read, or draw pictures in their tablets.

"Are so many people in Westby Catholic?" asked Silje.

"No," answered Millie laughing. "Only a few are Catholic. The rest of the kids go to the instruction so they can get outside and fool around."

"But they have to go to the church and listen, don't they?"

"Yes, but the boys, especially, think that's a small price to pay for being able to run around outside and tease the girls on the way," said Trina. "And the priest wants to convert as many people as he can to being Catholic. It gets him points with God or something."

"Has he ever converted anyone?"

Trina and Millie giggled. "If that ever happened, the Lutherans would stop letting them use their basement for the classes, and the instruction would end, because the Catholic church is outside of town and too far to walk to," said Trina.

"And Mr. Butter would lose his Thursday afternoon sleep time," whispered Millie. Mr. Butter had disappeared as soon as the release-time students left. Miss Cline was grading papers at the table in the front of the room ignoring the girls.

Silje liked Trina and Millie who seemed to be best friends. They seemed like such a mismatched pair: Millie a nervous girl with large blue eyes who might have been pretty had it not been for thin hair and a severe case of acne, and

Trina, kind of cute with her heart-shaped face and down-to-earth demeanor. Trina was shorter than both Silje and Millie. From them she was able to get occasional math tips to help her figure out how to do the problems that were so puzzling to her. Little by little, as the weeks went by, Silje had brought her math grade up from an 'F' to a 'D' and her goal was now to get 'Cs' on her homework by Christmas. The teachers offered no help; they seemed to assume that she was one of the dumb ones in the class of which there were several, mostly boys.

Clara had paired up with another girl, Mary Sveum, and they were sitting whispering together toward the back of the room. Another pair of girls, large Ann and skinny Dorothy, seemed not to relate to anyone else in the class, but at least had each other. Earlier, Mary had told Silje that they belonged to some kind of strange religious group in town that had built the basement of a church and then ran out of money to finish it. "Nobody knows what they do in there," said Mary. "Nobody dares to ask them. We just stay away."

Silje stood outside after school with a group of girls waiting for her mother to come and pick her up. A light drizzle had turned snow into slush; she hadn't ridden her bike since the end of October.

"Oh no, I forgot my book bag," lamented Mary. "I don't want to run all the way up to get it." Mary was chubby and flat-footed.

"I'll go get it." said Silje, setting her book bag on a damp spot on the sidewalk. "Watch my bag for me." She ran quickly into the school and up the three flights of stairs to the classroom. Mary's bag was nowhere to be seen. The room was empty. The teachers were gone and the lights were off leaving the room with only the dim light from the overcast sky filtering in through gloomy disconsolate unhelpful windows. Silje walked through the home room into the darkened classroom, flicked on the light and spotted Mary's book bag beneath the hook where her coat had hung. She grabbed the bag, turned off the light, and hurried down the stairs, hoping her mother hadn't shown up yet.

The group of girls was still standing where Silje had left them. "Here," she said. "Your bag was in the classroom."

The girls burst out laughing, Clara the loudest. Mary accepted her bag and turned back to the group. Just then Silje's mother drove up and honked the horn. Shocked at the response to her offer of help, Silje walked to car and got in. The girls were still giggling.

They're laughing at me. I got Mary's book bag for her, and they just laughed. She's fat and ugly and doesn't walk fast, and SHE laughed at

ME!!! What did I do wrong? Maybe I wasn't supposed to offer to help. Maybe kids don't help each other at this school. It's Clara's fault. She's the one who laughed the loudest. She's probably the one who laughed first and made the other kids laugh too. I hate her. I hate her with my whole being. I hate Clara Mitby from the bottom of my soul! Just wait. I will never offer to help ever again. I don't care what happens to any of you, so don't ask me for help, ever. If you need it, I will turn my head away, just like the moron Mary did.

The two of them were silent on the way home. Pauline asked how school had been just like she always did, and Silje answered, "Fine," just as she always did. Both were lost in their own thoughts for the rest of the ride. Pauline pulled the car off the highway, over the railroad tracks and down the long driveway to the front of the house; Silje got out and walked inside while her mother parked the car in front of the garage.

Silje felt the heaviness in her chest, and the deepening sorrow in her mind. She heard her own breathing and her own footsteps through the silent living room as she walked into her bedroom and set down her book bag. She didn't cry. She couldn't. Like many Norwegian-American children in this community, she had lost that ability long ago. "Get over it!" her mother had said to her again and again when she was upset.

"Cry baby! Cry baby!" Children yelled at any younger child that was reduced to weeping for any reason at all: falling down and getting hurt, losing at a game, being pushed aside by siblings. You learned to bury your feelings and not let them show. You learned to smile and even laugh no matter how you really felt.

It's all right. I learned something today, and that's the good part: don't trust anybody! I thought Mary would be glad that someone got her bag for her so she wouldn't have to climb the stairs all the way up to the classroom to look for it. I didn't mind going. I can run much faster than she can. And maybe she was glad, but wouldn't show it as long as she was with Clara. Mary is Clara's friend, not mine. They deserve each other.

I don't have any friends. Oh yes, Trina and Millie are friendly to me, but they both live in town and have known each other all through grade school. They play together after school and on weekends when I'm not there. Ma thought that I'd make friends this year to help me when I got to high school, but it's not working out. Maybe I'll always be alone. Maybe I'll never have any friends. That weird girl in seventh grade across the aisle from me keeps trying to be my friend, but nobody even in her own grade wants to be her friend, so I'm sure not going to. Fine. I'll just be by myself. I don't need anybody else. I hate them all!

"I'm going down the barn now to help Pa with the milking." called out Silje's mother from the kitchen. Silje heard her pulling on her rubber overshoes and then opening the door to go out.

"Wait!" said Silje. "I'm coming too."

Finally the bleak winter ended, and Silje could ride her bicycle back and forth to school. It gave her some freedom to hang out in downtown Westby with Trina and Millie before heading home. They walked up and down the aisles in the dry goods store to see if any new merchandise had come in. Sometimes, if any of them had some coins, they went to the drugstore's soda fountain and got an ice cream cone or a candy bar.

Though never getting a math grade above a 'C', Silje was doing well in all other subjects. Mr. Butter even read one of her papers to the whole class and said it was the best one that had been turned in that year. Her classmates seemed to see her differently after that; she didn't feel as if they treated her as one of the class idiots anymore.

5

Stalked

It was 1949, the summer of polio, and fear was everywhere. Parents kept their children close. Towns did not schedule summer group events and activities for their citizens. Those larger municipalities that had newly-built outdoor swimming pools closed them. People stayed home, and in Westby, farm families no longer flocked to town on Friday nights to shop, drink coffee together, and walk up and down Main Street seeing who else was in town. The small movie theater closed for the summer, just at the time when it was most needed by teenagers who had nothing to do.

Silje didn't know much about polio except what she overheard when her mother and Aunt Minnie talked about it. Sometimes she listened when Ma talked on the phone. They were still on a party line with six other families, and even though the farm wives tried not to listen to each other's conversations, the temptation was sometimes too great not to succumb. Whenever one family got a call, all other families on the line could hear the unique ring. Silje's family code was three short rings. Auntie's code was one long and three shorts. Those on the party line could turn the crank on their own wall phones to call each other, or if someone outside the party line was calling, "Central" would ring the appropriate code to connect them. Either way, anyone on the party line who was near their phone, could hear which one of them was getting a call.

Ma seemed to be on the phone more than usual. Silje suddenly realized that women on the line were talking together three and even four at a time. Privacy had disappeared. They no longer even pretended not to listen in to each other's conversations. If Ma heard a ring from the phone, she went to pick it up no matter whose code it was. She joined in as if that was the new norm of behavior, as apparently it was, at least for now. That's how Silje learned that polio had come to Westby; she heard her mother discussing it with the neighbors on the phone. But then, it had nothing to do with her, so why worry. *I've got bigger worries. Confirmation classes will start in a few weeks, and I have to take them at the minister's house with Cashton kids again. Groan. I don't even like them. Ellen is stuck-up, and Ralph is boring. It seems like I'm always the one left out no matter where I go, but Ellen and Ralph don't talk to each other either, so that's good. If all three of us don't like each other, at least that makes us all equal. Thank you God.*

Silje walked outside past the two horses tethered temporarily on the lawn and stopped briefly to watch kittens romping among their hoofs while mama cat sat nearby licking herself. *Get your babies outta there! Don't you care if they get stomped on?* Silje watched one horse step nonchalantly to the side just missing a kitten. *Oh my gosh! He just missed it! The horse must have sensed that the kitten was under him. How did he know the kitten was there? He never looked down or around.* Silje continued watching, and sure enough, no matter where either of the horses stepped to graze at a different patch of grass, they avoided stepping on the kittens that played happily about their hooves, just a squish away from certain death. *Amazing. Just amazing. . . there's more to animals than we think.*

"C'mon Pal. Let's go across the road and see if the cherries are getting ripe." Silje and her young cousin Robbie had discovered a cherry tree last summer on the far side of the patch of woods across the highway from their farm. This woods was part of the Reiersen farm, but when the highway had been built, this land had been cut off from the rest making it useless for development. It was used as a dump site by the former owners. Pal came running to follow Silje and to run ahead of her trying to determine where she was going next.

They walked up the driveway, crossed the railroad tracks and walked down to the edge of the highway. Silje called to Pal to sit beside her while a green pickup truck approached. The truck slowed, and the driver seemed to watch her as he passed by. A car came from the other direction, the pickup truck speeded up, and both disappeared.

"Okay. Let's go," said Silje, crossing the highway into the lane to the dump site. "We have to climb over this stuff to get to the tree. Tires, rusty machinery, old pails and cans, wooden beams, and things that had no definable use had been tossed into a deep hole and discarded items had spilled above and beyond it. Silje was careful not to cut her bare legs on the sharp edges sticking up. Once on the other side, it wasn't far to the tree. There was no path, so she avoided the burning-grass and hoped that there wasn't any poison ivy here as she pushed her way through the weeds.

Small cherries were beginning to form on the branches of the single tree, but it would be late summer or early fall before she could come back and gather some to taste or perhaps to take home and make a pie. Robbie hadn't liked them because they were sour and wormy, but Silje had picked out the worms and took tiny bites to avoid any worms she'd missed. It might be too much work to de-worm enough cherries for a pie. Maybe Ma would help.

Summer passed slowly. Silje helped her father out in the fields, and when she couldn't get out of it, helped her mother in the house. Boxes of books came in the mail every few weeks from the Madison City Library which she and her mother devoured, sent back, and waited for the next batch to come. Her mother chose the books from a list that came with the box, always including at least one or two romances by Grace Livingston Hill, her favorite author. There was no objection to Silje reading these books when her mother was finished with them, and from them, Silje began to get a picture of what idealized romance looked like and the obstacles that needed to be overcome to achieve the always happy outcomes. *Interesting, but sometimes the characters make stupid choices. I'll never do what they do.*

Silje drew pictures. She built little houses and carts from the wooden orange crates that her father gave her. She played by the pond beyond the sheds trying to sneak up on frogs before they jumped back into the water. One day she saw a huge snapping turtle crawling slowly toward the pond. Where had it come from? Her father said, "Stay away from it and leave it alone. It has its own life to live."

Salvation came in late July, when one day, Ma got a phone call from Trina's mother asking if Silje could come with them to their cabin in northern Wisconsin for a couple of weeks. The cabin was way out in the country on the shore of a small lake surrounded by forest and several miles from the nearest small town. There weren't any children anywhere near them so there should be no danger from polio.

"Do you want to go?" asked Ma.

"Yes! Yes! YES!" screamed Silje.

"How will we find our way back?" asked Silje, walking with Trina into the woods behind the cabin.

"Dad showed me how to tie white twine to the branches where we can always see at least two of them. Then we can follow them all the way back to the cabin. We can go as far as we want that way. Here, you carry the drinks and I'll tie the string." Trina used her pocketknife to cut a long piece of twine, putting the ball of twine on the ground while she tied the string on a branch creating a limp bow. Their progress wasn't fast, but speed was not the point. They had all day to explore the woods, and the day after, and the day after that.

This forest of tall trees was so different from the two small woods on the Reiersen farm. Where there was much underbrush on the farm, there was little here. It seemed as if the sun was blocked out by the tall trees, leaving the ground covered with old sticks, leaves, and general forest debris. Walking was easy although Silje could see that even just out of sight of the cabin, it would be easy to get turned around and lose one's way. It might even be hard to use the sun as a compass since not much light shown through to the forest floor.

"Why didn't Millie come?" asked Silje. "Did you invite her?"

"She came once a few years ago, but she got so homesick that her parents had to come and get her, and she never wanted to try it again. She gets sick easily and is afraid to be away from her mom."

"So you just come with your folks?"

"Yeah. It's not so bad. Dad and I go fishing every day, and I help him and Mom fix things. Something always happens during the winter that needs repairing. But I'm so glad that you could come. It'll be a lot more fun with you here."

The two girls could hear birds calling back and forth high in the trees, and a raucous noise just above them. "Must be a crow," said Trina.

Silje laughed. "No, it's a couple of squirrels having a quarrel. You must hear them in Westby. They're all around."

"Yes, but I always thought the sound was from crows. They're all around too."

"Caw, caw," shouted Silje trying her best to imitate a crow. Trina laughed and joined in. They tried to imitate other bird sounds, but collapsed in laughter at their pathetic attempts.

"Are there animals in the woods up here?"

"Just small ones. Rabbits, squirrels, chipmunks, things like that. Mom doesn't like it when mice come into the cabin. We try to keep them out, but they always seem to find a way in. I've seen snakes in the water. We've never seen anything bigger than that except neighbors' dogs that sometimes wander about, but they know us and are friendly. Why? Are you afraid?"

"No, just wondering. I didn't want to run into a bear!"

Trina laughed. "Let me tell you the story of the three bears," she said. She began, "Once upon a time there were three bears. . . ." Now you take the next part.

"One of the bears wore a plaid shirt and always carried a two-headed axe as he rode his big blue ox over tall mountains."

Trina chimed in, "The second bear had a large stomach, a bald head, and taught American history to eighth graders." Silje screamed with laughter as Trina stopped to tie another string around a branch.

"Can we see the last string? Oh, there it is," said Silje looking back. She began describing the third bear and stopped mid-sentence.

"Keep going," said Trina. "This sounds good."

"No. Listen," she whispered.

"What? I don't hear anything"

"I know. Neither do I. The birds have stopped singing. I don't hear the squirrels anymore."

"So what?"

"Something's wrong."

"Stop it, Silje. You're just trying to scare me."

"No, I wouldn't do that. We've gotta go back. C'mon." Silje turned around and headed back the way they had come. "Come on!"

Trina followed, protesting. "Silje, we don't need to go back yet. We have plenty of string to tie on the trees." She tossed the ball of twine up into the air, tried to catch it and missed. She turned back to retrieve the ball from the ground behind her, and that's when she saw it: a tawny shape lurking among the trees almost out of sight, but watching her. She froze. "Silje," she whispered. "Look! It's a huge cat. It's over there."

Silje looked toward where Trina was staring, and with some effort she, too, saw the large animal well-camouflaged in the minimal foliage. "Oh my gosh! It's a cougar, a mountain lion. I saw one in a cage at the county fair last year. There was a guy there telling how he caught it."

"Run! Run!" yelled Trina beginning to move.

Grabbing the shorter girl's arm as she tried to run past her, Silje said, "No! We can't run."

"It'll kill us!" Trina cried, panicking, trying to pull out of Silje's grasp. "We'll get eaten!"

"If we run, it will chase us, and it can run faster than we can. We're too far away from the cabin to make it back without it catching us." Giving Trina a hard shake while holding firmly to her arm, then slipping her grasp down to her wrist where she could hold her fast to keep her from running, Silje said, "We have to outsmart it. That's the only way. Climbing a tree won't help. It can climb better than we can. Begin walking. Now. Walk backward toward the last string."

Silje could sense the fear and panic in her friend. She was afraid too, but had never felt panic, ever in her life, except when those invisible hands had held her shoulders down, but that was different. That had been something she couldn't see. Not even when that stupid goat at her grandpa's farm had trapped her in a cow's stanchion and tried to butt her to death with his horns. It was like something took over in her mind at times like that. It was like time stopped and allowed her space to think of a way out. That's what was happening now.

"Trina, you walk frontward and guide us back along the strings. I'll walk sideways and keep an eye on the cougar so he doesn't come close. We'll walk fast, but we can't run! We mustn't run!" Still holding Trina tight, Silje nudged her forward. The girls moved at a quick walking pace toward each string visible at a far tree. Silje could see the flaw in the string idea. They were using a heavy twine, but even so, in this shadowy forest, it wasn't thick enough to see easily, and further, once they stepped out of the line of sight of the last twine, even just a few steps to the side, they could become hopelessly lost. She had to count on Trina to find their way home. Hopefully the strings were close enough together and the bows large enough to find quickly.

For a while, the big cat seemed to have disappeared. Silje couldn't spot him. *Maybe he went away. Maybe he's not there anymore. Maybe he isn't real. Maybe we just thought we saw a mountain lion. It was our imagination.* Then she saw him over in the trees creeping along keeping pace with them. *He's stalking us! Oh my god! God. God, keep us safe. Please. Make that cougar go away.*

"Trina, we've got to make noise. We have to sound fierce, like we're bigger than he is. Maybe we can scare him away."

Trina was half sobbing as she led Silje from string to string. "We shouldn't have gone so far," she said. "I'm sorry, Silje. This is my fault. I wanted to have a big adventure in the forest, especially since you were here. I would never have done this alone."

"It's okay, Trina. We'll get out of this. Don't worry. C'mon, let's sing 'Ninety-nine Bottles of Beer on the Wall' as loud as we can. When you think we're close to the cabin, start shouting for your dad to come and find us." Silje began shouting and singing 'Ninety-nine Bottles of Beer on the Wall' with Trina joining in to finish the verse. Then 'Ninety-eight Bottles,' and 'Ninety-seven Bottles,' growing hoarse with their shouting.

"Is it still there?" asked Trina just before beginning 'Eighty-seven Bottles of Beer on the Wall.'

"Yeah, but he's not coming any closer. He's following and watching us. We're okay. Keep singing!"

Finally, at 'Sixty-five Bottles of Beer on the Wall,' the girls began to smell the lake, and they knew they were close. Trina shouted for her dad to come and get them. She screamed for her mother, as she tried to run, but Silje held on tightly watching the cougar moving closer to them. If they ran now, the cat would surely jump them. Trina's voice was filled with the panic of being almost safe, but not safe. Silje was sure that the cougar sensed the girls' fear. Their bravado was gone; their voices and movements demonstrated it clearly to the cat. He was only four trees away now and still stalking. At any time he would crouch, run, and jump. *Please God. Make Trina's father hear us. Make him come. Now. We need help now! Please.*

As long as she lived, Silje would never forget the relief she felt at hearing the deep baritone voice of Trina's father as he walked toward them through the woods from the cabin just behind him. "Trina! Silje! Is something wrong? Girls! I'm coming."

As soon as he came into sight, Silje let go of Trina's wrist and let her run sobbing into her father's arms. She turned to look for the big cat, but it was gone. *We made it! Thank you God. You led us home.* She collapsed on her hands and knees, and then flat on the ground staying there until Trina and her father pulled her up stumbling forward barely able to walk.

Trina's mom was clearly shaken as she listened to their tale of outsmarting the cougar. "Never again, can you go into those woods without your father! I had no idea that these animals were anywhere near." The girls had changed their clothing and examined themselves for ticks. They were brushing each other's hair to be sure that none of the bloodsucking bugs had attached themselves on their heads or behind their ears.

"There was a mountain lion down near Coon Valley a couple of summers ago," said Silje. I went with my pa and my uncle to see the cow that it had attacked. It must have gotten scared off by the dogs, but it had jumped a cow in the barnyard during the night and left deep claw marks sliding down its back where it must have tried to hang on. The cow was okay though. The farmer kept it in a pen near the barn for a while so that everyone could go and look at it."

"They're not seen often, in fact rarely," said Trina's father. "I'll go into town tomorrow and alert the sheriff that there's one in the neighborhood. Since this cat is prowling during the day, there might be something wrong with it. Maybe they'll get a hunting party together to see if they can find and kill it."

"Can we come too?" asked Trina.

"We'll all go," answered her mom. "And for the rest of our vacation, we'll do lots of fishing and boating and canoeing. We're staying on the water. No more forest!"

6

The Man in the Balcony

Oh my gosh! I never dreamed that high school would be so much fun! I love it. Everybody even likes me! Well, a lot of the girls like me, and some of the boys notice me. Even though I wear glasses, it doesn't matter. Lots of kids wear them. And nobody knows about my false teeth; I'll never never tell anyone! If a boy ever kisses me, I wonder if he'll be able to tell. That could be embarrassing. I'll have to figure out a way so he won't know.

Years ago, when Silje was in sixth grade, all of her front upper teeth had to be pulled due to open decay and bleeding. She was fitted with a removable plate that she sucked up into the top of her mouth to keep it from falling down. It had become such a habit to constantly keep her teeth sucked tight that she barely noticed doing it anymore. Of course there was a thin gold wire around an existing tooth that helped to hold her plate in place too, but it was often lose and couldn't be counted on to keep the teeth from slipping. There were lots of snapshots of a younger Silje smiling and laughing with her mouth closed to hide her decaying teeth. What a blessing it was to not be afraid of freely laughing out loud along with everyone else. *Thank you God.*

Six red, white, and blue school buses were lined up in front of the high school waiting to collect the teenagers living on farms far away from Westby. The buses were identical, and over time, the kids intuitively recognized the nuances of the differing wear and tear on the buses to get on the right one, but some just looked for the bus drivers standing by the door of their bus waiting to check which students were boarding their bus and which were absent that day. It was easier.

Silje got on the Coon Valley bus and slipped into a seat next to Lou Ann, a senior who seemed to be almost the last person anyone wanted to sit next to. Silje remembered Lou Ann from Homestead Grade School, but there had been too many years between them to form any kind of a friendship. Silje didn't mind Lou Ann's awkward ways and felt a bit sorry that everyone avoided her, but nevertheless the chronic bad breath made even her shrink as far away as possible on this uncomfortable thinly cushioned seat. Silje sat quietly, and kept her head turned away.

"Are you getting off the bus to walk?" asked Lou Ann.

"I don't know. Are you?"

"Might as well. It's easier than riding the route all the way around. There aren't too many that do it this year. Last year there were a lot of kids, but most of them graduated."

"Okay. Let's."

Being the last one picked up by the bus in the morning allowed Silje to sleep later than the students picked up first on the route, but that meant she was the last one off after school in late afternoon having to endure more than an hour's ride over bumpy country roads in this old rattle-trap of a bus. The bus drove west through the hills and valleys toward Coon Valley letting a couple of students off at their homes before slowing to a crawl at the top of a hill with a gravel road leading down-ward.

"Anybody getting off?" asked the driver.

"We are," called Silje, Lou Ann, and a couple of boys who lived on Rongstad Ridge toward the end of the route. The bus stopped and the door opened

Clara almost never rode the bus after school, so Silje felt safe from having to endure her constant ridiculing giggle that always seemed to be aimed at her.

Silje and Lou Ann walked behind the boys who paid no attention to them; still it was comforting to know that they were in a group. "Have you always gotten off the bus here?" asked Silje.

"Most of the time, yes. In the winter it gets harder. We don't get off unless the road has been plowed. If the boys decide to tease the girls, we get into big snowball fights on the way down the road."

"There aren't any farmhouses along here," said Silje, thinking of last summer's cougar. "Anything could happen. What if a big animal came? What would we do?"

"It's never happened, so why worry?"

Just then a pickup truck drove past them kicking up a cloud of dust. The boys held up their middle fingers and yelled, "Fuckin' jerk!" The girls laughed, and the four began walking together to the bottom of the hill.

Basketball season began, and the first home game was this evening in the high school gym. Silje stopped at the bus after school to tell the driver that she wasn't going to ride home today. "There's a game tonight, and I want to go," she said.

"Yeah, I'll be here after the game to take kids home that don't have another ride," he said. "The buses will line up down there outside the bus garage. Come and get on right away after the game, or I'll leave you here overnight in the snow. Don't dilly-dally!" Blaine the driver was Silje's third cousin somehow or other, but it seemed as if she must be related to half the people in this county, so she didn't even try to keep track. Her mother did plenty of that, and Silje tuned her out when she began one of her monologues about who married whom and how they were therefore related to a hundred other people or maybe at least a thousand. The worst part was when she began naming them. *Help! Where's the nearest exit?*

"Come on, Silje!" called a group of girls. "We're going down town."

Silje ran to catch up with them. Alice and Caroline from the La Farge bus route had become two of her closest friends at school: Alice, a thoughtful dependable girl, and Caroline, a bit more daring. With them were the two tall skinny buddies Julie and Sally from just outside of Coon Valley. Both Julie and Sally rode the Coon Valley school bus, but lived after the hill where students got off to walk. The town kids went home before the games, but the kids from the country hung around downtown walking the streets in little groups, or when the weather was bad moving in and out of the stores and restaurants to keep warm and dry. Clara ran to join the group also.

Even if Clara is with us, it's so much fun being in a group of friends. Nobody knows how much I hate Clara, and even she doesn't seem to notice, and I guess she wouldn't since I either avoid her or put up with her. She even seeks me out sometimes as if we are friends. Little does she know! It has been easier since we started high school since there are so many kids around. She doesn't target me as much with her jibes and laughing. Maybe she doesn't dare since I have more friends than she does.

Walking through the slush on the sidewalks and sliding over the icy patches, the girls laughed and talked about teachers and classes and gossiped about classmates. "I think Thora is sleeping with someone," said Caroline.

"How do you know?" asked Silje.

"I don't know for sure, but I saw a pack of condoms in her purse. Why would she have them otherwise?"

"What are condoms?" asked Julie.

Thanks for asking, Julie. I didn't want to sound dumb, especially in front of Clara the snake.

"They're little rubber things that boys put over their ding-dongs before they have sex with a girl."

"Oh," said Julie. "How do you know that stuff?"

"My brother George talks about it. He says he's never used them, but all the boys have them just in case."

"Just in case, what?" asked Sally.

"Just in case a girl lets them make love to her," answered Caroline. "Boys always want to be ready for it."

"Eeeuuw!" said Alice and Julie together. "That's gross!"

Just then the sound of a car squealing its tires sounded behind them as it pulled sharply out of the street they had just crossed. Voices yelling and shouting. The girls turned their heads to see the commotion.

"Hey!" "Sexy bitches! Whoooooo!" "Have a present!!" the boys yelled as they drove past throwing something white out of the window.

The girls shrank back from the item until they realized what it was. "Oh my gosh!" said Caroline. 'It's a Kotex pad!"

"Eeeuuw!" cried Alice and Julie looking up to see the car rounding the corner. Edwin was waving a box of Kotex out the window while Freddie tossed another pad at girls walking up ahead.

"What are they doing?!?" said Silje.

"Just being stupid. Edwin probably stole the Kotex box from his mother, and now they're all having fun with it," said Caroline. "Ignore them, if they come around again. Pretend we don't see them. They're so dumb that they probably don't even know what Kotex is used for."

Silje guffawed. "That's like when Curtis tapped me on the shoulder in home room and asked me what a bra was. He didn't know!"

"What did you tell him," laughed Sally.

"I could tell he was really embarrassed, so I just told him that it was underwear that women wore around their chests. He didn't ask anymore, so I just turned back around and ignored him."

"Curtis is cute," said Julie. "Does he go out with girls yet?"

"Nah. None of the freshman boys do. Anyway, most of them are too short," said Caroline. "Who would want them?"

The car with loudly shouting town boys zoomed past them again. This time another boy was waving the Kotex box, but it was empty. "Wanna meet me after the game?" he called to anyone who would look at him. "Come on. I'll show you paradise!" Silje and her friends turned their heads away until the car had passed and watched it slow down slightly at the next group of girls walking towards downtown. Wanda, a town girl was with them and she held up her middle finger toward the boys that she knew so well from past school years. The boys screamed with laughter and drove on.

The bleachers in the gym were jammed with high school students, parents, city officials, and just about anybody who was a local sports fan, all waiting for the game to begin. Viroqua fans, who seemed to think that Westby was their greatest rival, filled the bleachers on the opposite side of the gymnasium from the Westby students and supporters. Occasional cat calls rose above the din whenever a student thought that no teachers or officials would see who did it.

The Westby players ran in a line into the gym from the door on the left of the stage to take their places, and the fans burst into shouting and waving wildly. The Viroqua players ran in from the door on the right of the stage to noise equally as loud from their fans. As fast as the noise had erupted, it quieted down as the loudspeaker announced the singing of the national anthem. Everyone stood and put their right hand over their heart facing the American flag on the stage as music from the loudspeaker led the singing. As soon as it finished, the players were out on the floor beginning the game.

It was hard at first to pay attention to the game. Silje was sure that she wasn't the only one totally fascinated by the legs emanating downward from the tiny basketball shorts barely covering the buttocks of the players. *How can they even hide their private parts in shorts so short? I'd be embarrassed to appear in public with that much showing. Oh my gosh, you can see some of the boys' lumps sticking out in the front of their shorts.* Nevertheless, she was captivated by watching the boys' legs and comparing their length and thickness and muscles with one another and choosing which she like the best. Not until second quarter, did she become engrossed in the game itself which moved fast, shot after shot, first one side ahead and then the other. The audience was wild with yelling and screaming.

During half-time, the girls kept their seats so nobody would crowd them out. "Did you see that guy up in the balcony?" asked Clara.

"What guy?" asked Silje.

"Right up there, next to the people wearing orange sweatshirts." The seat was empty.

"I don't see anyone," said Silje.

"He was there. Maybe he'll come back. Wait, there he is leaving the balcony."

Silje looked up. "So what about him?"

"He was staring at us, the whole time during the first half. He didn't watch the game at all. It was weird."

"Well, maybe he can't get over our amazing beauty!" said Silje turning away.

"No, it wasn't like that. He was staring just at us. He never turned his eyes away." But Silje was no longer listening. Caroline was talking about the dark-haired basketball player and how she wanted him to notice her. Most of the players were juniors and seniors so the girls knew they had no chance. Even in the hallways between classes, the upperclassmen averted their eyes from the younger students as if they weren't occupying the same space. Silje had begun watching a tall skinny player, aloof and seemingly mysterious, but oh, how he could shoot baskets. Most of the scoring was his. She sighed. It was the beginning of a crush, and she had no idea what she would do if he noticed her back.

7

Archie

Funny thing about disappearances. There was that girl down by Clockmaker School last year that no one ever saw again. Personally, I think it was a big cat that got her. A cougar probably. It would have dragged her away and eaten her completely, no trace to be found. Then Luke, the boy that sat in right in front of me all through eighth grade; he didn't show up for high school because he died of polio last summer. So I guess it was a serious disease after all. I'm glad I didn't catch it. Thank you God.

And now Tom Galstad's little brother Archie. Oh my gosh! Tom saw him being taken right after school and couldn't run fast enough to catch the man who drove away with Archie in the trunk. He could hear Archie screaming and pounding on the inside of the trunk lid, but they disappeared around the corner, and Tom couldn't catch up.

Law enforcement in Vernon County in the early 1950s consisted of one sheriff, one deputy sheriff, and numerous volunteers trained as needed for specific tasks. Like so many counties, the budget didn't support a well-staffed department of professionals, and the two men housed on the second floor of the county courthouse in Viroqua worked out efficient methods to try and maintain order in their jurisdiction.

Sheriff Joe Iverson had been a young state trooper when he answered the call to become the interim sheriff in Vernon County after its previous sheriff had died of natural causes. He found that he liked the work, ran for the upcoming election, and won the vote in that election and every one since. Though a well-trained professional, he would never have been able to handle this job had it not been for the deputy that he'd inherited. As different from each other as two colleagues could be, the two men found that they complimented each other's skills. Tall and lanky, Iverson was smart, analytical, and always probing for details. He was a problem-solver who did not stop until he had the answers.

Deputy Otto Bakke was a hulking giant of a man, lumbering when he walked, but surprisingly quick when needed. A gentle man and generally well-liked, Bakke didn't hesitate to intimidate with his large size. When he stepped toward a perceived offender and changed his facial expression to one of cold impersonal business, nobody wanted to do anything but cooperate.

Sheriff Joe Iverson happened to be in his Viroqua office when the call came from the Galstads that their youngest son had been taken. Too hysterical to give any details, Mrs. Galstad turned the phone over to her older son Tom who was still breathing hard from running home. "What happened?" asked the sheriff.

"There was a man. He took Archie."

"How did he take him?"

"He picked him up and threw him in the trunk and drove away."

"What did the car look like? Did you get a license number?"

"No, but the car was black. It was an old two-door coupe with a big trunk. It might have been a Plymouth, but I'm not sure." Tom's voice broke.

"Hold on, son. A couple of more things I need to know; you're doing fine. Did you see the man?"

"Yes."

"What did he look like? Can you describe him?"

"He was wearing jeans and a winter jacket. He had a cap with ear flaps. He looked kind of skinny and not real tall. But he must have been really strong to pick up Archie that way. Archie may be only six, but he's big for his age."

"What direction did the car go?"

"He drove to the end of our block and turned north."

"You did well, Tom. When your dad comes home, tell him that we'll start looking right away, but I want him to get as many men together as he can to help us. Can you do that?"

"Yes," whispered Tom.

"All right. Good. I'll be at your house in about half an hour to organize the search party."

With no way to communicate among the searchers, Sheriff Iverson and Deputy Sheriff Otto Bakke organized the men out of both Westby and Viroqua with two men to a car and sent the cars out in pairs along the highways and major country roads. If they saw a black coupe with a single male driver, they were deputized to stop the car and search it and especially to open the trunk. If nothing was found, they were to record the name and address of the driver and the license plate of the car, let him go, and continue to search. If it appeared that the driver was armed, they were to follow at a distance until they reached a telephone and call the sheriff's office with the location. They were all to meet back at the sheriff's office in the Viroqua courthouse by ten o'clock that night.

They found nothing. Archie was gone. The frustration and fear among the searchers when they returned to the courthouse was almost palpable. All had hoped that one of the search teams out there on the country roads had caught the kidnaper and rescued Archie, but the kidnaper must have had too much of a head start. Galstad had been in one of the cars searching from Westby, and when he heard that nobody had found Archie, he broke down in deep sobs, something that Norwegian-Americans never did. "How can I tell my wife? he said. "How can I tell Tom? Where is my son? Who has him?"

Because so many men from both Westby and Viroqua and the areas immediately surrounding these municipalities had assisted in the search, word spread quickly about the abduction. People talked about the young girl that had been taken more than a year ago and wondered if the two kidnapings were related. Sheriff Iverson reviewed the previous case also and re-interviewed the family, but concluded that the circumstances were different enough that there might be two different kidnappers in the area. What was going on? Child abductions happened from time to time, but this was a first for Vernon County. In all his years in office, he had never had a kidnaping that he couldn't solve. The few that had taken place had been done by relatives or boyfriends or someone who knew the victim. All the victims had been rescued and the kidnapers arrested.

This was different. This could be a stranger, someone that nobody knew. Sheriff Iverson was on the phone every day thereafter calling the sheriffs of surrounding counties and then counties further away throughout Wisconsin to gather information about abductions that might have taken place within the last two years. Then he contacted the larger municipalities throughout the state, LaCrosse, Madison, Milwaukee, and others. He was slowly putting together a card file of kidnapings, solved and unsolved. Patterns were beginning to emerge.

****

Archie felt cramped inside the car trunk. He pulled a bunch of oily rags under his head so that it wouldn't bump on the floor so hard. Turning on his side and putting his arms under his head helped too. Where was he being taken? The smell of gas exhaust was getting worse and making him feel dizzy.

He kicked at the trunk lid and yelled, "Let me outta here!"

"Shut up!" the man yelled back.

He can hear me, thought Archie. He began kicking the lid of the trunk and yelling and hollering as loud as he could.

"I gotta pee!" he shouted. "Let me out." He felt the car slowing and turning off gravel and onto something softer. The engine shut down, the car door opened and then closed.

Archie heard footsteps coming toward the back of the car. What was the man going to do to him? He rolled into a ball and pushed himself as far back into the trunk as he could. The cracks of light coming in around the edges of the trunk's lid suddenly grew large and blinded Archie's eyes as the trunk lid opened wide. The man was silhouetted against the sky as he looked down at him.

"Did you pee in my car?" the man demanded.

Archie didn't answer. The man reached into the trunk, grabbed Archie's jacket and pulled him toward the opening. "Let me see," he said, running his hands between Archie's legs to see if there was wetness on his blue corduroy pants.

"Get out," he muttered, lifting him up and out onto the side of the road. "Pull your pants down and do your business. Hurry up."

Archie stood a few feet away from the man and began slowly lowering his pants. How could he get away? He didn't want to go into that trunk again. He wanted to go home.

The man turned away from Archie, pulled his own zipper open and his flaccid penis out. He let out a forceful stream of urine toward the ditch next to the car.

Archie bolted!

Down into the ditch and up the other side, he scrambled away from the man. He rolled under the four-strand barbed-wire fence, got up running and headed through the empty pasture toward the woods on the other side, running as he had never run before. He heard the man shouting as he got his clothing caught in the barbs of the fence and heard him swear. Without looking back, Archie ran toward the woods. He heard the man running after him now, but Archie had a good head start. He tore into the bushes and trees not caring about bugs or spiders or scratches on his hands and face.

He's going to catch me! He's going to catch me! Archie fell to his knees and rolled under a thicket, curling up into a tight ball. He lay still. He heard the man's footsteps nearby and then further away, then nearer again. He was searching for Archie. Closing his eyes, Archie pushed himself further into the thicket. *If I don't move, if I don't look, he won't find me.*

He heard the man calling to him. "I know you're here, you goddamn stupid little shit! I'll find you. When I do, you won't know what hit you! I'll give you a whipping like you've never had before. Just wait. Just wait. I'll find you." The voice trailed off as the man moved away deeper into the woods.

Archie felt a warm stream of liquid escape between his legs and he began to cry softly, but he lay still, not moving, and made his whimpers quiet down as he waited for the man to come around again. He was sure the man was out there, just waiting for him to make a sound. This patch of woods was deathly still. The birds were quiet. A squirrel made his raspy sound once in a tree above Archie and then no more. The only sound was the far-off footsteps and the muttering of the man looking for him as he slapped bushes and poked underneath them with a branch that he had picked up.

When Archie awoke, it was dark. Something was crawling on his face. He brushed it off as he became aware of all the noises around him. Leaves rustled and an occasional twig snapped. A furry animal brushed past him and then ran quickly away when Archie moved.

What had been a gentle breeze during the afternoon was growing into a strong wind, and Archie could hear the branches of trees blowing back and forth above him. He was cold, shivering. Soon the noise became deafening as raindrops began to fall, just a drizzle at first and then a full downpour. He could see flashes of light and heard the rolling thunder right before the next flash, brighter this time.

A huge clap of thunder and the sudden brilliance of light all around him accompanied the loudest noise Archie had ever heard, hurting his ears. Lightening had struck a tree somewhere in the woods nearby.

Sobbing openly now, Archie pushed himself as deeply into and under the thicket as he dared where the rain and wind couldn't reach him. He curled up tightly to try and stay warm. Is the man still out there? *Is he still looking for me? Maybe the lightning struck him. God, please send the man away. Please. Mommy, come and find me. Mummy.*

When Archie awoke again, a big spider was weaving a web above his head. The rain had stopped, and it seemed as if maybe there might be sunshine somewhere. Without thinking, he crawled out from under the thick bushes and stood up. He felt cold and damp in his light jacket. He saw nothing but trees and foliage. He took a few steps, and then began to walk. He looked down and saw a couple of red berries that looked like strawberries. He picked them, put them in his mouth and squeezed the flavorful juice from the berries before he swallowed. He saw another one and ate that too. He was hungry. *Mommy.*

Far off, the sound of a tractor working a field grew louder. Archie pushed his way through the foliage until he came to where the bushes and weeds disappeared and there were only trees. He could see through to the edge of the woods, and walking became easier. Archie saw the tractor as he emerged from under the trees and ran toward it. He tripped on a clod of dirt, fell, and sat up crying. Tears were running down his face when he heard the tractor pull up beside him and stop, felt himself being lifted up into powerful arms, and heard a voice saying, "Well, what do we have here?!? Where did you come from, young feller?"

8

Things That We Can't See

One last confirmation class before the questioning. Silje sat close to the door on the passenger side of the car and gazed outside as the old Packard sped along. Pa said nothing as he drove her to the Cashton parsonage where the classes had been held every Saturday for the past year except at Christmas and Easter. If the three pupils didn't understand Luther's Small Catechism by now, they wouldn't be confirmed as members of the Evangelical Lutheran Church.

Has anyone ever failed to be confirmed? What if I miss a question? They said that last year, the kids had to stand up in the aisle between the pews while Pastor Martin walked back and forth asking each of them the questions. What if I die during the questioning??

"Ma will come and pick you up when it's over," Pa said as he pulled to a stop in front of the pastor's house.

"Okay," muttered Silje. *I hate this. Pastor Martin doesn't like me, I can tell. He's cold to all of us, but he pays more attention to Ellen. Ralph is either dumb or he never bothers to do the memorizing that we're supposed to do.*

She walked up the steps and across the porch. The door opened before she could knock. Silje turned and waved to Pa as he drove away from the curb and then followed Mrs. Martin into the minister's study. *Thank goodness I'm not the first one here.*

Ellen and Ralph watched her as she crossed in front of them and sat down in the row of three chairs facing the minister's desk. No one spoke. The large grandfather clock chimed nine times and then continued its loud tick-tock as the pastor cleared his throat and began to speak over the oppressive ticking.

"On Wednesday evening at the catechism, I will ask each of you one question from The Ten Commandments, The Creed, and The Lord's Prayer. You will answer the question and explain what the answer means when I ask you to do so. There will be no questions about baptism, communion, confession, or daily prayers. We'll go over those today so that each of you has a thorough understanding of their place in the church. Let us begin."

The minister kept his students past the time when the class should have been finished, so Ma was waiting outside on the porch with the other parents. "How was it?" she asked as Silje followed her to the car.

"Fine," growled Silje. Ma started the engine, and as they pulled onto Highway 27, Silje said, "I've decided. I don't want to be confirmed. I'm not going!"

"Don't be silly," answered her mother.

Every pew in the sanctuary of the church on Wednesday night was filled as Silje, Ellen, and Ralph walked single file up the center aisle toward the front. All eyes were on them. Pastor Martin stopped them in the aisle, introduced the three confirmands to the audience, and invited everyone to come back on Sunday to witness the Confirmation when these young people would join the church and be welcomed at the communion table as adult members of the Evangelical Lutheran Church. The questioning began.

Silje got the first one.

"What is the Second Commandment?"

"Thou shalt not take the name of the Lord thy God in vain," answered Silje.

"What does this mean?"

"We should fear and love God that we may not curse, swear, use witchcraft, lie, or deceive by His name, but call upon it in every trouble, pray, praise, and give thanks."

Ellen got the second question and answered it perfectly as Silje had done.

Then came Ralph's turn. The minister gave him questions with shorter answers and a few hints to get him through. That worked well for The Ten Commandment questions, but the answers for The Creed were long and convoluted, so while the pastor made Silje and Ellen each recite an entire article with its meaning, he seemed to forget to ask Ralph the meaning if he at least got most of the article itself correct.

The Lord's Prayer was more difficult still. The whole point of Luther's Small Catechism was to make adults and children alike memorize-memorize-memorize so that God's expectations would become ingrained in their souls and they would never forget their obligations and how to behave in a way that was pleasing to God.

"What is The Third Petition?" asked the pastor.

"Thy will be done on earth as it is in heaven," answered Silje.

"What does this mean?"

"The good and gracious will of God is done indeed without our prayer, but we pray in this petition that it may be done among us also."

"How is this done?"

"When God breaks and hinders every evil counsel and will which would not let us hallow the name of God nor let His kingdom come, such as the will of the devil, the world, and our flesh; but strengthens and keeps us steadfast in His Word and in faith unto our end. This is His gracious and good will." Silje quickly looked down as the minister stepped away toward Ellen.

I'm done! I'm done! That was my last question! It's all over except for Sunday. I did it! I can't believe I got everything right. It seemed like I couldn't get any of it memorized. Ma's advice worked: Do a little at a time and repeat what you'd done every time you added something new. Yes! Now I can forget it all! It's over!

Silje paid no attention as Ellen answered her question from The Lord's Prayer until suddenly a small commotion interrupted her perfect answer. Ralph had toppled over in a faint. The man in the pew next to Ralph was standing caught him before he fell to the floor, set him down into the pew, and pushed his head down between his knees. He and the woman next to him held Ralph there until he could stand up again.

The pastor ended the questioning without making Ralph answer his final question. After repeating the invitation for everyone present to come back on Sunday to watch the three take their Confirmation vows, the pastor gave a closing prayer, the words to which Silje heard none, and the congregation was free to leave. Silje felt as if a weight had been lifted from her, sort of like when the invisible hands had lifted up off her shoulders down in the woods that time, sort of like that, but not really.

There are people here in the church, lots of people. In the woods it had been just me. I felt so alone, but I wasn't alone, was I. Something else was there too, something watching me, something that didn't want me there. It made a mud hole and tried to make me disappear into it. When I got out, it tried to hold me down. I get scared every time I think about it. I'll never forget it, ever!

God, there are things in this world that we can't see. If you are omnipotent like the minister says, then get rid of these evil things. If you are omniscient like he says, then you know perfectly well what's going on here. So tell us. We need to know.

Silje lay awake in bed that night listening to the sounds of her parents moving around in the kitchen and then in their bedroom getting ready for bed. She hadn't experienced the mind-trick for a long time where her thoughts told her that her parents or other people were going to kill her. That seemed to be gone, but often when any grownups stayed for a meal with her parents, she filled her plate and went into her bedroom to eat. It was too hard to be around people with whom she didn't know how to talk. There were other things too.

She felt uneasy in a lighted room at night where a stranger in the darkness outside might be looking in and watching her. When riding in a car, she held her breath and sometimes even closed her eyes if the car passed under a bridge or overpass, relieved when it didn't fall down crushing her while she was beneath.

Worst of all was her fear of spiders. Silje had a clear memory of when it must have begun. She was sitting in a highchair while her mother and her aunt Minnie were working in the kitchen. They were still living together then, two families in one household. Ma and Auntie were talking nonstop as usual. Suddenly a huge black spider crawled onto the tray of the highchair. Silje remembered screaming and pushing at the tray trying to escape. She tried pulling herself up out of the chair, but she was trapped. The monster spider took a few steps toward her. Silje, crying and screaming, finally felt her mother turn towards her and take notice. Ma scooped the spider into her hand, threw it on the floor, stepped on it and went back to her conversation with Auntie. Silje was left to herself in the high chair, her crying finally subsiding into whimpers.

It doesn't seem possible that people could remember something from when they were so young, but I remember something even earlier. It's weird. I remember looking up and seeing a pale lightness that didn't change no matter how I jerked my head back and forth. Worse was the terrible, inescapable smell that surrounded me. That's it. That's the memory. What it was, I have no idea, but it's there, and sometimes it comes back to me, like now.

Silje's thoughts drifted as she waited for sleep to overtake her. *I understand The Ten Commandments and The Lord's Prayer. They make sense. Of course there have to be rules for how we act toward each other and toward God. What I don't get is The Creed. It seems like somebody, probably Martin Luther, just made that up. If Jesus really descended into hell, how would anyone know that anyway. Did someone see it happen? What if they lied and we kept on believing it ever after.*

And if Jesus delivers us from all sins, why did Archie get taken? Why did he have to spend a whole night in the woods by himself, under a bush in a terrible rainstorm hiding from a kidnapper? Something is definitely wrong here.

"You can't get off the bus anymore," shouted Blaine the bus driver, turning his head only slightly and glancing at the students in the rear-view mirror. It wasn't wise to take one's eyes off these narrow gravel country roads. "Everyone has to stay on until they get off at their own place." He drove quickly past the entrance to the road at the top of the hill where the group of students usually got off to walk down to the valley to wait for the bus to return from its Coon Valley run.

"Noooo!" yelled several teenagers. "We won't get taken. Don't worry. We've got enough big kids with us to fight off any kidnaper"

"It's not going to happen, not to us!"

"We can't sit on this bus for a whole hour all the way to Coon Valley and back. Our butts will get all shook off; our bones will rattle, our brains will fall out!" the teens yelled at Blaine and laughed at each other.

"Sorry," said Blaine. "Orders are orders, and I wouldn't stop even if I was still allowed to." He refused to respond further to their shouted complaints and eventually it died down to grumbles, mutters, and other topics.

I'm glad that we can't get off anymore even though it's been a ton of fun fooling around with the bus kids on the hill. If we were still able to get off, I would have to do it too or be called a chicken. I'll bet everyone is as relieved as I am though nobody would admit it in a million years. Everybody is scared. Everybody. Kids can't play outside anymore unless there is an adult watch-

ing them. What fun is that? But it's better than being kidnaped and never seen again, and we all understand that.

Still I think it's more dangerous for us country kids than the town kids. We have to get off the bus and walk a ways to get into our houses. Some kids have mothers who come out to the mailbox to meet their kids every day, but lots of us don't.

What if someone is watching?

****

After his return home, Archie slept between his mom and dad in their bed for a couple of nights before deciding himself to go back to his own room. Every night for about a week after, his brother Tom dragged a blanket and pillow to sleep on the floor next to Archie's bed ready to be there comforting him when he awoke after a nightmare.

Perhaps what helped Archie the most was what Sheriff Joe Iverson did. The sheriff waited until Archie had been home for two days before going to the house to question him. With Tom and their parents present in the room, the sheriff led Archie step by step through what he remembered of his experience: being thrown in the trunk of a car, what he had heard during the ride, the escape into the woods, and the man looking for him as it grew dark.

Even though he didn't need to hear the rest, Sheriff Iverson continued to lead Archie through his night sleeping under the bushes, what he had heard and felt: the furry animal and the bugs. They didn't talk about how scared he'd been. They didn't have to.

With the family quietly listening, the sheriff led Archie to remember the morning walk out of the woods, eating the wild strawberries, and the breakfast of pancakes and syrup prepared for him by the farmer's wife. He remembered the farmer turning the crank on a wall phone and talking to someone, and sitting on the lady's lap while they all rode in a brown sheriff-car to a place where he finally saw his mom, dad, and Tom again.

The sheriff of Trempealeau County had met Sheriff Iverson and Archie's family at La-Crosse where the handover occurred. The two sheriffs talked for a few minutes, discussing how they might work together in tracking and catching these child abductors. They speculated that there was something bigger going on here than isolated kidnappers working alone. The two men promised to keep in touch.

As Sheriff Iverson got ready to leave the Galstad's home after interviewing Archie, he turned to Archie and said, "You did well, Archie.

You did everything just right. Tell you what, when you are all grown up, you come see me, and I'll make you a deputy sheriff!"

9

Beneath the Illusion

Summer came and went. There had been so much to do. Yes, she still had to help her parents on the farm especially in the tobacco fields: planting, hoeing, picking off the caterpillars, chopping, piling, spearing, and loading. Raising tobacco was all hands-on work, and since it was in addition to the ongoing farm activities that supported the dairy cows from which their regular income came, there was little rest for farmers.

Yet, teenagers found time to connect with one another. Silje had made friends in high school, and they tied up the country telephone lines with their phone calls back and forth. Other families who shared these party lines often picked up their telephone receivers intending to make a call, only to hear girly chatter. When told to hang up, the girls quickly ended their conversations. A few hours later, they'd be talking again. Telephones seemed to be addictive for teenage girls.

That summer, Silje discovered that boys might actually be attracted to her, well, one boy at least. He was her age but a year behind her in school in the grade where Silje should have been had her parents not started her in first grade at Homestead School when she was five. Brian was taller than Silje, had curly hair and blue eyes that crinkled when he smiled, but she noticed all that later when she first saw him in the light.

"May I?" he said, sliding past her knees and into the seat beside her just as Charlie Chan entered a darkened alley up on the movie screen. Silje didn't answer. Neither said anything to the other as they watched the old Chinese detective plod through the scenes solving this most recent heinous crime.

The movie ended, the lights came on, and Silje noticed that Brian followed close behind her as they walked in the crowd up the aisle and through the small lobby. Once outside, she looked around for her parents.

"Maybe I'll see you next Friday night, mumbled Brian as he pushed his way past her. Silje turned and watched him walk away not looking back. She heard her father honk the horn as he drove up. She jumped into the back seat and pulled the door shut.

"How was the movie?" asked Ma.

"Fine," answered Silje.

She looked forward to Friday nights in town. Farmers and their families filled the sidewalks and stores, buying groceries and fancy baked goods, replacing broken tools, and talking with relatives and neighbors. The sidewalk along Main Street was crowded as were the side streets leading off to other small shops.

Main Street itself roared with cars driven back and forth by older teenage boys showing off their manliness by how many girls they could entice to take a ride with them. Older high school girls walked in groups at the outer edge of sidewalks hoping to be invited for a ride. Only the most daring would enter a car driven by the long-haired duck-tailed Viroqua boys that drove the ten miles to Westby, probably because Viroqua girls shunned them.

Sometimes when Ma and Pa were busy having coffee and doughnuts at Borgen's Café with lots of other people, they gave Silje money for the movie. She'd buy her ticket, get a bag of popcorn, and find a seat about half way down the aisle on the left side. Soon, Brian would slip into the seat next to her, and they would hold hands and whisper about the story unfolding on the screen. Roy Rogers was Silje's favorite, but Brian liked Randolph Scott. As soon as the movie was over, they would separate immediately to find their parents who never knew about this very first ill-fated romance.

One Friday evening in August as they left the theater, Brian whispered to Silje, "I'll see you in high school if not before."

Oh my gosh! He thinks I'm his girlfriend! Oh no. No, no, no. I can't be seen in front of my friends in high school having a boyfriend who is a freshman! No way. What am I going to do?

Silje stopped going to the movies on Friday nights and stayed close to her parents unless she saw one of her younger cousins. Then she might switch families and walk with them for a while.

It wasn't hard to avoid Brian once school began. They had different schedules, different home rooms, and if he tried to approach her in the halls between classes, she was friendly but distant. They rode on different buses and soon it was clear to Brian that they had gone their separate ways.

Sophomore year was good. Silje played alto saxophone in the band, found that she loved algebra, and got mostly Bs with an occasional A or C. Her name was listed on the Honorable Mention sheets posted each month, and once her name even made it onto the Honors list. History was boring, English was easy, and she was consistently vying with a red-haired junior student for the top spot on the typing tests. Silje never met Brita as she was in another class, but if she saw that Brita was listed first on the bulletin board list, Silje doubled her efforts to beat her the next time. It was a silent unspoken competition between the two of them, and one that nobody else noticed except maybe the teacher who must have been delighted.

Best of all, Blaine the bus driver was letting the students off the bus at the top of the hill again, but only if there were at least five of them and if they promised to walk in a group. The Archie incident had happened more than a year ago and nobody was thinking about it anymore. Archie had come back, hadn't he? No tragedy there.

One afternoon toward the end of April, Silje got off the bus, waved to Blaine as he drove away, and trudged up the incline toward the railroad tracks running past the farm. She walked over the tracks and around the bend toward the house. She stopped, put her book bag down on the grass by the side of the driveway, removed her jacket, and picked up the bag again. Not too heavy today. Just some problems in algebra and she could do those in the morning before catching the bus. The dog got up from his nap and came to greet her.

"Hi Pal. Did you miss me?" Silje walked up the porch steps and into the kitchen. "Ma?" No answer. The house was silent.

Silje took her book bag into her room, tossed it on the bed and went back into the kitchen to see what was there to eat. A torn piece of paper lying on the kitchen table caught her attention.

"We went to LaCrosse," it said. Her mother's Palmer-Method handwriting was neat and precise, much better than Silje had ever mastered. Silje cut two slices of bread, went to the refrigerator and took out the butter and strawberry jam. With a paring knife, she cut slivers of the rock-hard butter across both slices, and covered them with the sweet lumpy jam. She returned the butter and jam to the refrigerator and went outside. With the dog following, she wandered around the yard munching her sandwich. Needing something to drink, she gave the crust to Pal and went back inside. *Boring.*

Why did they have to go to LaCrosse today? Why didn't they wait until Saturday when I could have gone with them?

Silje poured a glass of milk for herself and turned on the radio. She didn't care about all the afternoon programs for kids anymore, but listened to 'The Lone Ranger' anyway. It was something to do. When it ended, she turned off the radio.

I need to hear when they come home. What if someone else drives in before Ma and Pa get here? What if it's a stranger, someone I don't know? Don't be stupid. Nobody is going to come at this time of the day. Everyone is in the barn milking cows.

Silje brought her book bag into the kitchen and laid out her homework on the table. Algebra was much more fun than arithmetic had ever been because it was logical. There was no memorizing anymore. All you had to do was figure out relationships. That was fun. There were more problems than she had realized, and by the time she finished, the sun was going down.

Good thing I did this now instead of waiting until morning. I might not have gotten it all done in time to turn it in.

Where are Ma and Pa anyway? They should be here by now? They have to come pretty soon to start the chores. Cows don't wait. That's what Pa always says.

She went outside to see if Pal was around. He was. She petted him, and he lay down again, unconcerned. It felt creepy being this alone out here. *What's wrong with me? I've been alone at home many times. It was never a big deal.*

"Here Pal. Come here." Silje went up the steps of the porch. "Come here. It's okay, boy." The dog followed her. He sometimes lay out on the porch waiting for someone to come out, so being on the porch was familiar. Silje opened the door to the kitchen. "Come on. Come inside." The dog hesitated. This was new, different.

"Come on. It's okay." The dog pushed past her and entered the kitchen. Silje closed the door.

Silje turned on a lamp in the living room and flopped down on the davenport to read. Pal wandered from room to room examining each new space, smelling the odors of the people who lived here. He lay down next to Silje and seemed to doze. It grew dark outside. *Where are they?*

Suddenly Pal lifted his head, got up and went into the kitchen. Silje followed. "What's the matter puppy-dog?" Even though Pal was now a large, grownup Collie mix, Silje still used the term of endearment that she'd given him when he was a little puppy yapping around her ankles.

Pal sat down by the door to the porch and looked back at Silje. "What's the matter? Don't you like it in here? Do you have to pee?" Pal got up, circled around Silje and sat down again by the door. "Oh, all right. You can go out." As she began to open the screen door, the dog pushed through, bounded off the porch, and disappeared into the gloom.

Silje pulled shut the screen door and pushed the single hook down into the ring on the door jamb. She closed the wooden inner door that held no lock. Rather than turning on the kitchen light, she flicked the switch to turn on the yard light. High on a pole halfway between the house and barn, the bright bulb illuminated the space between the buildings and shone dimly into the kitchen as well. Silje went back into the living room, but didn't feel like reading anymore. She turned off the lamp and went into her bedroom. The room was dark. Once in a while the lights from a car coming over the rise way out on the highway could be seen briefly through the north window, but it had nothing to do with her. Those cars were approaching from the wrong direction. None of them would be Ma and Pa. She lay down on the bed and curled up, but she was wide awake.

Where are they? Ma's note said they went to LaCrosse. It took less than two hours to drive to the city or back again. If they left LaCrosse by three, they should have been home by five. It was seven-thirty now. The cows will have come up from the pasture all by themselves. They were probably bawling their heads off in the barnyard wanting to get milked.

What if Ma and Pa don't come home? I can't milk twenty-three cows by myself. If they don't get milked, their udders will get too full and burst. They'll all die and it will be my fault. Pa will be so mad! Please, please come home.

Silje sat up on the bed and leaned her arms on the headboard gazing out the window. She counted the headlights of cars coming over the hill until she got bored doing it. Where was Pal? Should she bring him back into the house to keep her company? Ma told her once that it was all right to do that if she was home alone and got scared.

I'm not going back outside. Who knows what's out there? Too many shadows. Things hide in shadows. Where is Pal? He barked a while ago, but I haven't heard him again. Did something get him? What if he's gone? What if I'm alone?

Fear gripped her. She didn't move. Silence. She listened for any sound, any sound at all. . . . A slight rustle in the wall. That's just mice. The sound of the mouse was comforting somehow. It was real. It was familiar. *Just so it doesn't die in there, and we have to put up with the smell until the body dries up. Ugh.*

If Ma and Pa don't come home, what shall I do? I'll have to walk up to Auntie and Uncle's and tell them, but maybe they went to LaCrosse too. They might not be home either. I could walk over the Torkelson farm, but I don't know them very well. They've got only boys and they're still little. They're not relatives but they might help anyway. At least they'd know what I should do.

Please, please come home. NOW! Come home NOW! Silje closed her eyes. *When I open my eyes, I'll see the lights of our car coming into our driveway and they'll be here.* She opened her eyes. Nothing. Darkness. A breeze seemed to be starting up; she could see the silhouette of bushes swaying slightly against distant headlights.

What if it's not the wind? What if someone is out there? The front screen door is hooked, but there is no hook or lock on the side door off the living room. Silje made her way into the living room and propped a chair under the knob and hurried back to her bed. She felt like she was the only person left alive on the earth. *Is this how Archie felt when he was in the woods by himself? He wasn't alone though. A man was hunting him. He KNEW he wasn't alone! What if the kidnaper knows I'm alone and he's outside waiting. What if he killed my parents? What if they were in a car accident and are laying along the highway somewhere? What if they never come home? Ever. How will I manage? How will I get food to eat?*

She pulled the bedspread from the bed and wrapped herself into it. Just as she was settling back next to the window, she saw the lights of a car swing over the railroad tracks and come around the bend of the driveway. They were home.

Silje jumped off the bed, hurried to the living room, and pulled the chair from beneath the knob on the door and put it back where it belonged. She turned on the kitchen light, unhooked the screen door and went out onto the porch. Pal barked in greeting as he ran to the car and circled it as it parked in front of the garage.

Ma and Pa came up the porch steps and into the kitchen with Silje following.

"Why did it take you so long?" she whined. "You should have been home hours ago. I waited."

"We stopped for dinner in Coon Valley," said Ma. "We were hungry."

"Get changed," said Pa. "We've gotta get the cows milked."

"You too," said Ma to Silje. "You have to help. You don't need to change your clothes. Just go and set up the milk machines so that we can get started as soon as we get down in the barn. It's late, and we're tired."

Silje felt like crying as she and Pal walked toward the little milk house to assemble the machines. There were three sets that were taken apart, thoroughly washed and left to dry until the next milking. By the time Pa and Ma came to carry them into the barn, Silje was finished assembling the machines, and she walked alone back to the house.

They don't even care. They don't know how scared I was that I'd never ever see them again, and I'll never tell them. Never. I don't care. They'll never know.

A deep sorrow laid itself over the anger she felt at being left alone for so long. She was hungry, but didn't stop in the kitchen. In the bedroom, she stripped off her jeans, blouse, and underwear, and pulled her pajamas from the wardrobe in the corner. Crawling between the sheets, she pulled the covers over her head and left only her nose exposed so that she could breathe. A habit since early childhood, there was almost no surface area of skin for the random spider to find and bite her; especially she didn't want anything to crawl into her ears.

Silje dozed and then lost herself in sleep, but it was like there was an entire other world waiting there for her, and it wasn't a pleasant one. This night she experienced the first of the nightmares that would come almost every night for the next week. During the coming days she reflected on the dreams cementing them into her conscious memory never to be forgotten.

I don't get it. I've had nightmares before. Usually I barely remember them in the morning and forget what they were right away. This one is different. It starts out the same way every night, exactly the same. Then each night it goes further than the night before, like something was yet to happen, but doesn't.

I told Tillie about it when we were riding home on the bus, and she thought it was crazy. Maybe it won't come back. Maybe if I go through it in my mind, step-by-step, my mind will realize that it should stop doing this.

I'm in my bedroom at night. It's dark outside and I'm alone. I see a light somewhere in the yard so I look out. There's a large man with a jack-o-lantern head staring at me. His eyes and nose and mouth are glowing from the candle inside his head. He's very tall and his mouth has no teeth and he's grinning. That's all I remember from the first night. The second night he walks across the lawn toward my room. I'm alarmed, but not afraid. The doors are hooked and barricaded. He can't get in.

The following night, the pumpkin man comes closer, the doors fly open and he enters the house. I'm terrified as he appears in the doorway from the living room to my bedroom and stands there looking at me.

All of this happens again the next night, but this time he steps into the room. I run out of my bedroom through the door to my parent's empty bedroom. I hear him following me.

On each night thereafter, the dream continues to progress a little further, but just a little: I run through the kitchen; I'm outside waiting, thinking that he's gone; I see him come out of the house, and I run; he follows me into the backyard, I am running, he is walking slowly and steadily after me. When the nightmare finally stops coming at night, I have run out on Highway 27, and a car is coming toward me.

Silje was aware that the fear was back. The almost primordial fear that had gripped her as a small child apparently had never really left.

The fun and stability that she had found in high school was an illusion, a momentary break from the reality that was hers: the world in which she lived was impersonal. It didn't care. If there was anything good to come of her life, she had to find it on her own. She had to figure things out for herself as she went along, as events happened, as people tried to make her do what they wanted without regard to what she might want or need.

I can do this. I can find a way. Like Pollyanna, I can look for the good in all things that seem bad. I can try to help and not hurt the people around me. God, give me the strength to find my way.

10

Clara

Silje pulled her maroon one-piece gym suit up over her body and snapped the front shut. She hurried out of the locker room, through the basement tunnel and up the stairs to the gymnasium. She wanted to be among the first to get a basketball and begin practicing throws before Miss Pierce started class. A few had arrived before her, but she grabbed the last basketball and dribbled it to the far hoop where she got in a few attempts at sinking the ball before all the others came and she had to share.

Girls' basketball games were different from boys' in that there was a clear demarcation across the center width of the court that could not be breached without penalty. The six-on-six rules stated that each team had six players, three forwards and three guards. On one side of the demarcation, Team A had three forwards and Team B had three guards. On the opposite side of the court, Team B had three forwards and Team A had three guards. Any player could handle the ball, but could only dribble it twice before either shooting or passing to a teammate on either side of the line which they themselves could not cross.

"We're short one student today, so we'll spend some time in warm-up, and then we'll play with only two guards per team with one student floating between the teams and changing sides half-way through. Anybody know where Clara is? Is she just late, or is she absent today?"

"I think she's sick," muttered a student. A titter of giggles fluttered briefly through the group. Miss Pierce ignored them.

"Let's go! Line up! Run twice around the gym, and then we'll have some shooting practice before we play a game."

Silje sat in home room trying to complete a social studies assignment before having to turn it in to the teacher next hour. Social Studies was her last class on Tuesdays, and although she liked the teacher and found the subject interesting, she always became sleepy during the lecture. She finished the assignment and let her thoughts drift. *Should she or should she not break up with Charlie?* She'd been going out with him on Saturday nights for the past few months, but she was tiring of him. Yes, he was good-looking. Yes, he was fun to be with most of the time. Yes, he drove her to the wedding dances in Cashton that she loved, but he didn't dance and wouldn't try, so she had to hang out with her girlfriends waiting to be asked to dance by other boys while he stood on the sidelines with his buddies and watching.

He drinks too much, and he knows I don't like it. I've seen him drunk only once when he came to pick me up for a movie. I'm glad I didn't go with him that time. People shouldn't drive when they've had too much to drink. I don't think it's safe, but lots of men do it. Uncle does it, but Auntie doesn't say anything. I'm glad Pa doesn't. It's a good thing Pa didn't see Charlie that time.

I think I'll just stop going out with him. I know when he usually calls, so I'll be sure to go outside somewhere so I can't hear Ma calling me to the phone. I can go skating on the pond for a couple of hours. It's frozen solid now and way on the other side of the storage shed by the old tobacco barn. No way will I hear her calling me. That's what I'll do. If he comes around, I'll just be nice, but tell him I've got other things to do. If he's persistent, I'll just tell him that it was fun, but it's over.

The bus ride home was boring. The weather was too cold and windy to walk down the hill, so Silje rode around the entire route bouncing and jouncing on the hard leather seats. What little padding existed on the seats didn't help much. She didn't feel like joking with the other kids, so she sat alone looking out the window watching the fields and trees and farms roll by.

That evening, Sheriff Joe Iverson drove into their driveway. Alex quickly got up from the supper table and went outside before the sheriff got out of the car. Pal was barking and growling ready to attack anyone he didn't recognize. Silje and Pauline watched through the window as Pal calmed down willing to merely sniff at the sheriff as Pa greeted him and invited him inside. The sheriff briefly petted Pal, so that if he had to come again, he'd be recognized.

"No thanks. I don't need supper, but I'll have a cup of coffee if you have it made," said the sheriff stamping snow from his boots before entering the kitchen and wiping his feet on the rug by the door. "I'm here to talk with Silje," he said, sitting on the chair offered by Pauline.

Alex and Pauline looked at Silje with surprise as if she might have done something terrible. "No," she stammered. "I haven't done anything. . . ."

"I just need some information," said Sheriff Iverson taking a sip of coffee. "Silje, when was the last time that you saw Clara Mitby?"

"Clara!?" answered Silje surprised. "I don't know. Yesterday, I guess, in home room. We don't have many classes together this year. Why?"

"Did you see her today?"

“No, she wasn’t in school. I don’t think so anyway. She’s supposed to be in my physical education class, but she didn’t show up. Somebody said she was sick.”

“Do you remember who said that?”

“No. I didn’t pay any attention.”

“Does Clara ride the bus with you”?”

“Not always. Since she moved so close to town, she either rides her bike or she sometimes walks to school with her brother. She rarely rides in the afternoon because she’d be the last one off after me and it’s a long route. She gets home much faster by walking.”

“But she sometimes rides in the morning?”

“Only if it’s raining or especially cold like it was today.”

“So she might have waited for the bus today?”

“She wasn’t out there so Blaine didn’t slow down. She’s not signed up to ride the bus, but Blaine picks her up in the morning anyway if she’s waiting by the mailbox.”

“What happened?” asked Pauline. Is Clara all right?”

“We don’t know yet.” The sheriff finished his coffee and stood up. “Selma Mitby says her daughter walked out to the mailbox in the morning to catch the bus, so she thought Clara was in school all day. When she didn’t come home this afternoon, she waited until about six o'clock, and then she and Delling went looking for her."

"What about Paul? Doesn't he know where she is?" asked Silje.

"No. Paul car-pooled with another child in his class. He and Clara rarely see each other during the day since he's still at the elementary school. He knows nothing. He was crying when I left, obviously very scared." He paused. "No one that we spoke to in town saw her today, not in the stores or on the street. We're still contacting teachers and anyone who works at the high school.

Alex walked with the sheriff out to his car. Silje and her mother looked at each other with alarm.

"She was taken???" asked Silje.

"No, no. We don't know that. Don't worry. Clara will turn up." Pauline turned back to the kitchen table and began clearing the dishes from it. By the time Alex came back inside, Silje was in her room thoroughly shaken. She listened as Pa recounted his conversation with the sheriff.

"He says that we haven't had a kidnaping in Vernon County since Archie was taken, but they've been happening in other parts of Wisconsin. He's been keeping in contact with other county sheriffs. The state police are keeping close watch on this too. They think it could be a ring of child abductors out of Chicago or Minneapolis/St. Paul, but it's just a guess. Nobody knows.

Ma said something that Silje couldn't hear, and her parents continue taking in lowered voices.

Clara? Waiting for the bus? I wait for the school bus every day. All the country kids do. It could have been any of us. It could have been me!

Silje heard the kitchen door open and close and the Packard sedan's engine start. She looked out the window and saw the silhouette of her father in the car against the yard light as he drove toward the bend in the driveway and out to the highway.

"Where is Pa going?" asked Silje entering the kitchen and picking up a dish towel by the sink.

"To the Mitby's. He's going to see if he can help." Ma emptied the dish water into the sink, rinsed the pan, and dried it with another towel.

"But the sheriff said she's been gone all day," said Silje.

"They might want to start a search either tonight or tomorrow morning."

Silje and her mother walked back and forth drying the supper dishes and putting them in the cupboard saying little, each stunned by the horror of this latest possible kidnaping. Yes, it could have been Silje.

11

The Growing Void

The next morning, Silje stood by the railroad tracks at the top of the driveway's rise waiting for the school bus. She'd be able to see it coming, and she could run down to the highway to quickly jump on the bus when it pulled to a stop. Nobody would be able to snatch her then.

Shivering in the cold morning air, she watched one car and two pickups drive by before she spotted the bus coming over the hill in the distance. She picked up her schoolbag and walked down to the highway. The bus was packed with silent, still sleepy teenagers. Silje walked to the back of the bus as it pulled away and squeezed in with the boys in the back row. No one was allowed to stand in the aisle. Nobody spoke.

They don't know. None of them know yet that Clara has been taken. Silje said nothing.

The bus finally pulled to a stop in front of the high school in line with three other school buses discharging students from various parts of the countryside. Another bus pulled in and parked just behind.

The halls were crowded. Locker doors opened and slammed shut as students chatted and hurried to their first-period classes. Word was spreading fast about a missing child. Rumors flew among the boys and girls that someone had been kidnaped right here in Westby. Yesterday. Who? Don't know. Nah, you're thinking of the Galstad kid. No, someone else. Now. Yesterday. Can't be true.

About thirty seconds after the bell rang, just as all the students were settling into their seats, the principal's voice came over the loud-speaker: "There will be an assembly in the gymnasium immediately. The students in each classroom will march single file in an orderly fashion to the gym after their teachers and will sit together as a class. After the assembly, you will march back to your rooms and resume classes." The speaker clicked off.

"Leave your papers and books on your desks. We'll be coming back here. Row one, follow me, then each row follow in line," said Mr. Turner, the biology teacher.

Silje waited until the third row stood and began to move. She knew what the assembly was about and nodded when the boy in front of her turned around and said, "I heard it was Clara Mitby."

Silje whispered, "She was taken yesterday morning while waiting for the school bus."

"How do you know?"

"The sheriff came to our farm last night wanting to know if I'd seen her at school."

"Was she here?"

"No."

The normally raucous students filed quietly into the rows of chairs that had been hastily set up by the janitors that morning. It was clear that this was no ordinary assembly. The principal, assistant principal, Sheriff Joe Iverson, and his deputy Otto Bakke were all seated on the stage. The five bus drivers were standing at the back of the room. When the last of the students and teachers were seated, Principal Carlson got up to speak through a hand-held microphone attached by a cable to large speakers hanging on either side of the stage.

"Good morning," he called out.

"Good morning," answered the assembled students in unison.

"I first want to address the teachers. It is extremely important that you take attendance at the beginning of each class period throughout the day and send a runner with the information to my office as soon as these are complete. All the school bus drivers will also take attendance of students riding on the buses both morning and afternoon. If any of you students are not riding home on the bus after school for any reason, you must give a written permission slip from your parents to the driver. If anyone who is signed up for the bus does not show up, the drivers are instructed to report this to me before they leave on the afternoon route.

"Students who live here in town are to walk home in pairs or in groups wherever possible. In any case, by the end of the week, you will be given a list of names of people who have agreed to receive your telephone calls saying that you got home safely. Each of you will have a specific number to call. DO NOT fail to call. If the safety number has not been called by six o'clock each day, we will notify the sheriff.

"I know that you are wondering why we are taking these strict precautions. I'll let Sheriff Joe Iverson explain." Principal Carlson returned to his chair as the sheriff took the microphone from him and began to speak.

"Yesterday afternoon, I received a report that a student from this high school had not returned home after school. Upon investigation, it appears that this young woman had walked up to Highway 27 to wait for the school bus in the morning, but when the bus arrived, she was not there. Since she was only an occasional rider, the driver did not question her absence and proceeded to the school as usual. Her parents assumed that she was at school all day. Her teachers assumed that she was absent due to illness.

"We have had search parties out looking for her since yesterday evening, but so far, no trace has been found, and she is now officially listed as a missing person. Photos of the missing girl, Clara Mitby, have been sent to nearby counties and to the state troopers." Joe Iverson looked over the crowd of upturned faces staring at him. Seeing rapt attention, shock, and horror, he didn't want to frighten them unduly, but he did want them to take this absolutely seriously and elicit their cooperation in keeping themselves and their younger brothers and sisters safe. A few of the girls were crying.

"It is important that you pick up the flyers at the door as you leave, read them carefully, and share them with your parents and all members of your household. Your teachers will go over them with you in detail when you get back to your classrooms.

"In the coming days, teams of people will be sent to all the schools in Vernon County, both in the towns and in the rural schools to teach rules of safety to the children. Any questions?" As Sheriff Iverson turned to hand the microphone back to the principal, he noticed a lone hand raised up among the students. "Yes?" he said.

"Was she kidnaped?" asked a boy in the third row.

"We don't know what happened yet," answered the sheriff. "We're trying to find out where she is. It's possible that she has gone somewhere on her own and that she'll come back on her own. We hope that is the case. Nevertheless, this is the second disappearance in Vernon County in the past four years, and in addition there was one attempted kidnaping, so we are taking no chances. Follow the rules, and you'll be fine."

Sheriff Iverson handed the microphone to Principal Carlson who dismissed the assembled students back to their classes.

She's gone. Clara is gone. She's been taken! As she followed in the line of students filing out of the gymnasium, Silje noticed the people on the stage deep in conversation as if they were planning something. *Clara. Why did it have to be Clara?* Torn between her past dislike for Clara and her horror at what might be happening to her now, Silje felt a jumble of confused emotions. She wasn't the only one who hadn't liked Clara. Her bossy know-it-all ways alienated other students too, but Silje had gone out of her way to avoid the girl. She really hadn't liked her at all. Silje hadn't hated Clara; 'hate' was too strong a word, but she'd actively and knowingly disliked her intensely, and now there was a growing void in her mind where dislike-of-Clara had once had a home.

12

Teddy

The initial shock of Clara Mitby's disappearance dissipated as the Westby community began the last push to prepare for the annual Snowflake Ski Jump event in February. After all, nobody had really known the Mitbys very well. They weren't related to any of the large clusters of family groups that lived in the county, and they stayed to themselves most of the time.

Delling Mitby finally found steady work in Milwaukee; Selma was staying at their rented house so Paul could finish out the school year. Silje wondered if they had given up on finding Clara.

Clara, wherever you are, you'd better find your own way home, because nobody's looking for you anymore. If you do get back here and your parents have gone, you can stay at my house for a while. Yes, you can. It's okay. My folks won't mind. Then we'll find your parents, and they'll come and get you. They care. I know they do. Remember that wonderful cake your mother baked for your birthday when we were in seventh grade? That was a good party even if I had to leave early.

Alex had been at the ski jump down in Timber Coulee every day this week helping to pack down the snow on the jump's surface so that the ski jumpers could practice. Several Olympic competitors were coming again this year and would compete against the best of the local skiers as well as others from around the country who liked the Snowflake jump. A crowd of thousands was expected, so this completely volunteer organization wanted this event to go smoothly, to show the world that Westby was important, and its Norwegian-American citizens knew what they were doing. Pauline and Silje were baking sandbakkels and molasses cookies to sell at the food booth. Others were preparing barbecue beef sauce for the hamburgers and hot dogs that would be served. Still others were creating craft items to sell. This was to be a big year for starting to raise the money needed to build an even bigger and better ski jump in a few years. Silje, Caroline, and Alice had all volunteered to help sell in the booths on Friday evening and on Saturday. They wouldn't find out until the last minute whether or not they'd be assigned together or to separate tents scattered about the area. It didn't matter. It was exciting to be a part of such a huge event.

Silje ate dinner quickly on Friday; she and Pauline loaded the car with bags of sandbakkels and cookies and drove down to the ski hill. After unloading all the bags, Pauline left Silje at the main tent and went home to help Alex with the milking. Alex and Pauline would go back to watch the event the next day.

"Where do you want me to go?" asked Silje of an important-looking woman. "Are Caroline and Alice here yet? Can we be together?"

"You've been assigned to the drinks tent. It's over there near the foot of the jump," said the woman who seemed to be in charge. "All the supplies are there. Someone will tell you what to do."

Silje grabbed a sandbakkel and walked through the crowd of workers and early comers toward the drinks tent. A big sign above the tent said 'Drinks Here' Below was another sign listing coffee, cocoa, tea, and water, and the prices for each. She looked around for her friends, but didn't see them.

The ski hill and the valley below were well lit, and cars were pulling in, one after another, to the parking areas that had been plowed free of snow. The lots were filling fast, mostly with adults tonight, but tomorrow would see many families and lots of kids streaming into the valley around the jump. Because the ski jump was so high, it could be seen better in its entirety from further away, so onlookers felt no need to stand close by. Each skier could be seen pushing off the top of the jump, sailing down the slope of the jump before disappearing into the inverted arch and surfacing again at the lower tip of the jump before flying up, up, into the air off the jump itself, landing far down the hill and sliding into the large circle at the far end and skidding to a stop. Every year, there were skiers who attempted breathtaking feats such as somersaults in the air before landing on the slope below. It was a thrill to watch every time even when skiers fell, tumbling end over end into an undignified pile of man and ski poles.

Silje didn't see much of the jumping this evening. She hadn't considered that by volunteering to work in a service tent she'd be missing all the fun, and she hadn't laid eyes on either Caroline or Alice. She was so busy pouring hot beverages and making change that before she realized it, the evening's competition was over, and the crowd was dispersing.

This has to change. I'm not doing this tomorrow. I've gotta see Petter Hugsted jump. Silje headed over to the main tent to tell the boss that she couldn't help tomorrow. Caroline was there ahead of her talking with the woman in charge.

"I'm not feeling good," said Caroline. "I don't know if I can work tomorrow."

"Well, if you're sick, you're sick. Here's Silje. She can take your place at the crafts tent in the morning. It's only until eleven anyway, and then another crew comes on. We've got enough workers to cover the drinks tent, but only a couple for the craft tent, unless you'd rather do the food tent, Silje. We need people there too."

"No, um, I'll do crafts. It's okay. Only until eleven?"

"Yes, we wouldn't want to wear you out now, would we," she said laughing and turning away."

Silje and Caroline walked toward the parking lot. Lights on the hill were blinking out, leaving only a few to be left on throughout the night.

"Are you really sick?" asked Silje.

"Yeah, sort of," answered Caroline coughing lightly.

"You rat! You just didn't want to work tomorrow."

"If I'm feeling better, I might come and watch for a while," she giggled.

Silje picked up a hand full of snow and threw it at Caroline who ran away laughing. "Oh there are my folks. I have to go."

"See you tomorrow," yelled Caroline. "I'll stop by the craft tent at eleven and get you."

Working at the craft tent was easy compared to the drinks tent. Individuals and families stopped by to purchase a t-shirt or sweatshirt and occasionally a knit hat if they'd forgotten to wear one that morning. All the merchandise had a tag saying 'Snowflake Ski Club Westby Wisconsin and the clothing also had a snowflake woven above lettering 'Ski Club 1952.'

It was a very cold day even though the sun shone brightly in a cloudless sky. Hand knit scarves were selling well, being used to wrap around faces to keep cheeks and noses from getting frostbite. Breath steamed right through the woolen knit.

Children spotted the small rag dolls, handmade wearing snow pants and holding popsicle stick skis. "Please mommy, please," they begged. "Can I have one?"

The next shift of volunteer workers came just in time. Caroline yelled, "Come on, Silje. Petter Hugsted is next! He's about to kick off."

Silje tossed her Norski apron on the counter and ran after Caroline. "Money's in the pockets," she yelled back at her replacement in the tent.

The two girls pushed their way through the throngs of people. Spotting Alice near the wooden snow fence enclosing the landing site, they joined her. "Where were you?" asked Silje. "We didn't see you anywhere."

"I was in the food tent. Oh my gosh! I've been boiling wieners for two hours!"

Caroline laughed. "I saw you back there when I bought a hamburger a while ago. I didn't dare call out to you. I was afraid you'd throw a pot of boiling water at me."

"Caroline was so bored at the craft tent last night that she told the boss lady that she was sick and couldn't work today," explained Silje. "I took her place at crafts today, because they had enough volunteers at the drinks tent."

"We shouldn't have volunteered for this," said Alice. "Next year, the grownups can do it all."

"Oh, I don't know. It was kind of fun selling drinks. I really had to think fast when making change, because we had people lining up the whole night buying coffee and cocoa. Everyone was so cold. They were stamping their feet and jumping up and down just to keep their circulation going."

"And NOW!" said the announcer over the loudspeakers. "We have Petter Hugsted from Norway. Petter won the gold medal in the 1948 Olympics at St. Moritz, Switzerland. We are proud to have him here in Westby this year!" The crowd was silent, holding its collective breath. Those standing further up the valley could see all the jumpers push off the top of the huge structure to ski down the entire jump before sailing into the air over the hill. What they couldn't see was what Silje and her friends saw as they stood with the crowd at the bottom near the landing circle. Petter Hugsted was suddenly off the jump, into the air, soaring above them for what seem like forever, landing smoothly far down the slope, and skiing to a perfect stop near the fence where Silje and her friends stood.

The crowd roared its approval. The hero freed himself from his skis, and just before walking off the ski run, he turned toward the girls, grinned with half a smile, and winked.

"Ohhhhh! I'm going to die!" screamed Alice.

"He was winking at me!" yelled Caroline. "I know it!"

"No, me!" shouted Silje. "He looked at me! Right in my eyes! His eyes met mine!" They jumped up and down as the crowd around them laughed.

Normally taciturn and reserved, the Norwegian-Americans here today let go with an unrestrained enthusiasm that Silje had never before heard. She spotted her father through a brief opening in the crowd waving his arms; it looked like he was even shouting! *I've never seen that before. He never gets excited except when he's mad about something.* Silje lost sight of him as the crowd shifted, but the picture of her father so thrilled that he shouted and waved his arms would be burned on her memory forever. It was a side of him she'd never seen before, like he was a kid. *I suppose he actually was a kid once too. Never occurred to me. Amazing.*

"Teddy! Teddy! Where are you? Come here right now," a woman's voice shouted. "Teddy!" Her voice grew more shrill and panicked as she called. Silje saw a woman running toward them.

"Have you seen him?" Silje and Alice shook their heads.

"What does he look like?" asked Caroline. "We can help you look."

"He's four years old and he's wearing blue snow pants with a brown wool jacket. He's got a red Norski ski hat on his head."

"Oh, I remember you. I sold you that cap at the craft tent this morning. Come on," said Silje. "I know what he looks like. Caroline, if you go with Teddy's mom, Alice and I will go in the other direction." Caroline put her arm on the mother's shoulder and walked with her through the crowd calling for Teddy.

"Where is Teddy's father?" asked Caroline.

"He's still in the army in Korea," replied the woman. "Teddy!?! Oh God! Where is he?"

People in the crowd were turning away from watching the ski jumpers to begin calling for

Teddy. Some joined the search walking quickly through the crowd asking others if they had seen a lost little boy.

"He's been taken!" sobbed the mother. She leaned against Caroline. "He's been taken. Somebody's kidnaped my baby! Oh God, no!" The woman slid down onto the snow and continued to sob. What shall I do? I can't lose him! I can't lose him! What is Will going to say?"

Caroline could see the fear in the faces of the people gathered around her. "They're thinking what I'm thinking," she thought. "They're all thinking about Clara and about Archie. Maybe they're not talking about it anymore, but nobody has forgotten. Teddy could have been taken too." She saw a girl she recognized from high school with tears running down her face.

An older man broke through the crowd. "Come with me, Marjorie." He helped her to her feet. "We have to look for him. He's around here somewhere. He just wandered off." Caroline watched them walk slowly away, the mother crying softly.

"That's her father-in-law," said a voice. "Will's father."

"Teddy's grandpa," said another. Caroline heard people muttering about another child disappearing, taken this time because a foolish mother wasn't keeping an eye on her child. A commotion arose a few yards away, and Caroline saw Silje and Alice coming through the crowd.

"Guess where we found him," said Silje.

"Where?"

"At the food tent," answered Alice. "He was hungry, so we bought him a hot dog."

Teddy, smiling widely, had ketchup smeared over his chin and on his coat. "What's wrong, Mommy?" he said as he was lifted into his grandfather's arms. His mother, speechless, laughing and crying all at the same time, hugged them both.

"I think we'd better head home," said Grandpa. "Enough excitement for one day."

"NEXT, we have from Japan, Chokichi Satou, the SOMERSAULT KING!" said the announcer.

"Oh, we gotta see this!" said Caroline. "Let's get closer." The girls pushed closer to the red wooden snow fence encircling the landing area. "Here he comes!"

The Japanese skiers were back this year showing their incredible skills. They hadn't come to the 1948 jump competition as it had been too close to the end of the war and anger against them was still too raw. They were here now though and in better shape than ever. The first skier flew off the tip of the jump and immediately flipped over into a somersault before landing perfectly on the hill and skidding to a stop at the bottom. The crowd clapped, and only a few people turned away refusing to acknowledge him.

13

The Man in the Bleachers

The cold of winter finally faded into a wet and drippy spring. Alex was busy repairing and oiling the farm machinery so that it would be ready to use as soon as the weather warmed and dried enough to plow and prepare the fields for planting. Pauline continued to work side by side with Alex both morning and evening, feeding and milking the cows. Silje knew that she would be put to work as soon as school was out for the year, but right now, she was permitted to concentrate all her efforts on getting good grades at school, not like some of the boys whose grades suffered because they worked all year round leaving little time to do homework.

Silje's father Alex had passed sixth grade before dropping out of school, a decision he still regretted. He read fairly well, but his writing was poor, barely literate. Her mother Pauline had finished high school and gone on to graduate from the two-year 'normal' school in Viroqua preparing for her short career as a rural school teacher before getting married. To Alex especially, education seemed important, essential for managing even one's everyday life, and certainly one's future, because Pauline handled all the farm records and taxes, something that Alex could not do.

High school had become routine. Get out of bed. Finish homework. Eat breakfast. Walk out to the railroad tracks. Wait for the bus. Walk down to the highway. Get on the bus and squeeze in wherever she could find room. Ride silently the few miles into town to the school.

The school day became less bearable as the weather warmed and everyone longed to be outside. Lunchtime talk in the cafeteria was all about summer plans: who was going to do what—much of it wishful thinking.

"I can't wait for the roller skating rink to open."

"I want to go to LaCrosse to buy new clothes. Mine are all faded and worn out."

"Let's take the bus to Madison for a day. Then we can hang out at the university. Meet some cute boys."

"Why Madison" Let's go all the way to Milwaukee and stay overnight. I have an aunt who lives there. We could stay with her."

"I'm hoping there are lots of wedding dances in Cashton. I love those," said Silje.

"Who are you going to dance with? Charlie is long gone," said Alice.

"I'll dance with you!" laughed Silje. "Charlie never danced anyway. There'll be plenty of others. Remember those cute twins from up by Bangor?"

"Sexy!" answered Caroline. "I couldn't tell them apart though."

"One of them is a little taller and walks straighter than the other one. I'd take either one."

"Or both," said Alice. They all laughed.

Next year they would all be seniors. They would be the admired ones! Everyone in school looked up to senior students. They seemed mature, smart, sophisticated, and had put many of their silly hijinks behind them. Seniors paid little attention to the younger students, especially freshman and sophomores who acted so silly. Some juniors would still be accepted, especially those who dated seniors or those who rode the buses with seniors who lived out in the country. Tillie, a sophomore this year, rode Silje's bus and they had become good friends. But, as a rule, seniors wanted nothing more than to graduate and get out of high school. These students at the end of their junior year were already feeling it.

"This is so boring!" said Caroline. "I've got to get out of Westby."

"Me too," echoed Alice.

I have always wanted to leave here, ever since I can remember, but where would I go? I have no money and no way to earn a living. I could join the army, I suppose. No, the air force would be better. Their uniforms are blue. I look better in blue than brown.

The one thing I don't want to do is to marry a boy from around here and spend the rest of my life baking bread and milking cows. Ugh. And getting fat.

Silje shook herself out of her reverie and rose from the lunch table along with the other girls. Why did she feel guilty for wanting to leave? *Ma and Pa have each other, plus thousands of other relatives, and most live nearby. We're related to at least half the people in Vernon County in one way or another. I could go. They don't need me.*

"Don't forget the yearbook meeting in fourth period!" called Freddie as he rushed by.

"I'll be there," answered Silje, tossing a flirtatious cast of her eye toward him. Freddie, a tall good-looking boy with bedroom eyes had lured her up between the big boulders at the Westby park late one afternoon last fall. She had let him kiss her, but when his hand crept under her skirt, they'd had a little tussle, and she ran away laughing. Since then, Freddie had kidded around and flirted, but never tried to touch her again. She sometimes wondered how many other skirts he'd lifted. Silje had been kissed by other boys in her class too in private moments, but she always felt as if they were trying it out to see how it worked. Only Freddie had tried to go a little further. Boys could be so dumb!

After the next class, Silje stopped at the hall restroom just as Alice was coming out.

"Someone's in there throwing up," she said.

"Who?"

"Don't know. She's got the stall door shut, and she wouldn't answer when I asked if she needed help."

The restroom was quiet when Silje went in, although one of the stall doors was closed. Silje did her business, washed her hands and walked out. The hallway was almost empty as she hurried into her classroom. Just before entering history class, Silje turned to look back toward the restroom. Mary Jane Mason, a classmate that Silje didn't know well came out and hurried down the hall in the opposite direction, walking quickly. She didn't seem very sick, so Silje put it out of her mind. Maybe Alice got it wrong.

The buses were all lined up as usual when school got out. Just before Silje and Caroline headed toward separate buses, Caroline said, "Tomorrow, Westby is playing baseball at Viroqua, and I want to go to the game. Want to come with me?"

"What do you mean? It's during school."

"We could skip the last period and catch the Greyhound. We'd see most of the last half of the game. Come on. Nobody would know."

"I don't know . . . ," said Silje. "I've never skipped school before. What if someone misses us?"

"They won't. It's last period. We're in separate classrooms. The teachers don't even take attendance anymore. The boys on the team will be absent so the teachers won't notice that we're gone too. It'll be fun. Come on."

"Okay. Let's try it," said Silje.

"Bring some money for the bus," called Caroline as she walked quickly away.

The school day dragged on and on. Most days were like this now as April morphed into May, sunny, warm, pleasant, a perfect day for a baseball game. It wasn't fair that Viroqua students could catch part of the game during their free periods while the Westby team had nobody but a few parents to cheer them on. Silje hoped that she and Caroline wouldn't be recognized by anyone who might report them.

At 1:45 p.m. just before the last period began, Silje mingled in the hallway, put her books in her locker and walked out the front entrance of the school. Caroline was waiting.

"We have to walk close to the wall until we get to the east side so that no one can see us from the windows. Then we can run across the street and down the alley until we're out of sight of the school," whispered Caroline.

"Have you done this before?" asked Silje as they snuck along the wall.

"Sort of, but not really. I did a dry run once when I was thinking about skipping, but I never went through with it. George stopped me. We had a big fight about it." George was Caroline's older brother who often drove his sister and her friends to wedding dances in Cashton. He'd had a crush on Silje since the beginning of her sophomore year and sometimes worked up the courage to ask her to go out with him on a real date, just the two of them. Silje had always politely declined, making up some excuse that she hoped sounded legitimate. She genuinely liked George, but had no intention of getting involved with him in any romantic way. Sometimes Caroline had encouraged Silje to go out with George, and then it became a bit awkward, because the answer was still no.

"I don't want to get involved with my friends' brothers," Silje always said. "It just doesn't seem like a good idea." In truth, she didn't want to become close to anyone here in Westby. Her goal was to leave, period, and to leave no complicated attachments behind.

The Greyhound, with its engine running, was already parked in front of the drug store on Main Street as Silje and Caroline ran breathlessly up the steps and into the bus. They bought their tickets from the driver, and settled into a couple of plush seats toward the back. There weren't many passengers on the bus today, and they saw no one who might recognize them. With relief, they settled back into their seats while the bus pulled away from the curb.

"Caroline," said Silje. "Do you think all the kidnapings have stopped?"

"Don't know," answered Caroline after a pause. "I don't think about it much. Nobody I know was taken."

"What about Clara?"

"That's different. I didn't know her very well, and didn't like her at all. She was a bossy bitch." Caroline added, "Besides nobody's sure she was taken. Maybe she just ran away. Her father left, and her mother's leaving. I think they know something that the rest of us don't."

"Maybe," said Silje. "But I think she was taken. And I think the sheriff thinks so too.

Why, otherwise, would he have gotten together all the search parties?"

"So why did they stop searching? Maybe Sheriff Iverson knows something too. There is definitely something weird about the whole Clara thing."

"I don't know. It scares me. I do think about it and keep wondering who'll be next."

"Well forget about it for today. We're going to Viroqua to show support for our gorgeous, handsome baseball team!"

"And yell our heads off!"

"And help them win!"

"Just by being there!"

"And holler 'Go Ned' whenever he's up to bat!"

Silje laughed. "You've got a crush on Ned?"

"Who doesn't? He's the tallest, best-looking boy in our class. Every girl in school would like to go out with him."

"He's in band too, plays trumpet. He's really good."

"He's good at everything. None of us have a chance at going out with him. We've gotta stick to the country boys, Silje. I'm resigned," sighed Caroline.

The game was well underway when the girls climbed the bleachers and sat with the few people cheering for Westby. At an angle just on the other side of the batter, the bleachers were full of Viroqua students and parents yelling whenever their side was up to bat.

"Who's that guy?" said Silje pointing to a man seated on the plank a few rows beneath them.

"I've never seen him before. I don't think he's from Westby."

"What's he doing on our side of the bleachers?"

"Maybe he just wants to watch the game," said Caroline.

"I've seen him, but where?" muttered Silje. "I know I have. Wait until he turns around so I can see his full face."

Caroline was no longer listening. Ned was up to bat, hit a single, and ran to first. Silje yelled encouragement too, but turned her attention back to the stranger. The man rose from his seat, turned and climbed to the top of the bleachers to seat himself behind the girls.

Silje caught the man's eye briefly as he climbed past them. He looked directly at her, then at Caroline. It felt like he was appraising them, looking them over. She felt a chill, an internal alarm. *I recognize him. I've seen him. It was from afar, but I know I saw him somewhere. Think Silje, think! Where was it?*

The game continued, almost to the last inning now with Westby leading by only three runs, Viroqua going mad on their side of the bleachers. Silje watched, and yelled, and did all the things that she was expected to do as a loyal Westby team supporter, but inside, she was reviewing in her mind all the places where she might have seen this man. *This is important. I need to know. There is something wrong here. Friday nights in town–no. In the movie theater–no. It was in a crowd, I know. I remember that much. I saw him in a crowd of people. Where have I been in crowds? At the ski tournament–no. At the basketball games last fall and winter–no. Wait. There was the game where Clara was sure that a man was staring at her from the balcony across the way. I barely saw the guy she was pointing at before he left the balcony. Could it be him?*

As the baseball game ended with Westby winning to the applause of the parents and onlookers on the Westby side, Silje took advantage of the people standing and applauding to steal a look backward at the stranger. *It could be him. I can't be sure, but it could be the man who was watching Clara that night at the basketball game.*

"Come on, Silje," called Caroline hurrying off the bleachers. "Let's get a ride back to Westby on the team bus. They'll let us on. How can they say no?!?"

Silje jumped from plank to plank down the bleachers and onto the ground. She caught up with Caroline, and they ran to the school bus loading up with players. If they got back to Westby in time, they'd be able to catch their regular buses home since the bus drivers waited for the players to get back from the game. Some of the baseball players were country boys and had no other way to get home except by bus, so rather than have the buses do two trips round their routes, it was easier to wait the extra half hour or so for the team to arrive. Anyway, the bus that was being used to transport the team was one of the regular school buses, so as soon as it got back, it would fill up with students and head out on its regular run.

Silje forgot about the man on the bleachers as she flirted and chatted with the baseball players. They were in their dusty sweaty uniforms, and even though some of them were dorks in school, they all seemed like heroes today.

14

A Lucrative Business

The man whistled a tune with no melody. He used to whistle when he was a young boy, he remembered, mainly to show off to his younger brother who couldn't whistle at all. He smiled. This had been a good day. The two young children on the mattress in the back of the pickup had struggled, but neither had been a match for him.

They'd been playing by the side of a large shed out of sight of the house where presumably their mother was oblivious to the man in the bushes just off the country road next to the shed. Kidnaping children was so incredibly easy. He often wondered at it.

First he had enticed the younger child, a boy about four, by placing a bright-colored ball just inside a large stand of bushes a little ways away where the child could spot the color and come to see what it was. The girl happened to have her back turned when the man reached one long arm around the boy's head covering his mouth and the other arm grabbing the child's small body. In the flash of a second or two, tape covered the mouth, wrists and ankles of the child who was then thrust back further into the bushes where he couldn't be seen.

All the man had to do now was wait for the girl to come looking for her brother. It didn't take long.

"Willy!" she called. "Willy, where are you? Stop hiding. I know you're there." She walked toward the concealed man calling out as she walked. "Come out, or I'll go tell Mom that you've been naughty again."

Suddenly a man rose from behind a bush. Before she could react, he had taped her mouth and pushed her to the ground binding her ankles. He pulled her behind the bush, taped her wrists, and shoved her back with her brother. Then, still out of the sight line of the house, he walked through the brush up to the road to bring his dark green pickup closer to where he could easily load up the children. Not a soul saw him, not the mother in the house, not the father out in a field somewhere, and not a single vehicle had passed by. So easy.

It was late morning, and he could get back to Baraboo by early evening, but he hesitated in speeding up the pickup. He mused that the children would be rather hot under the plastic tarp. He'd drive in the shade as much as he could, and the breeze from the moving vehicle would help to keep them from overheating. With these kids, he'd have a full van of fourteen children to deliver. There were twelve currently locked in his basement waiting for him to come back so that they could have the run of the house again and make warm meals for themselves in his kitchen.

His children, for he thought of them as his own, at least temporarily, had acclimated well to their new situation. Some had been with him for several months and he had taught these early ones how to help the later ones to integrate into the household plan: to clean the house and the basement, to wash their own clothes and hang them out to dry on the line in the enclosed backyard. He gave them seeds so that they could plant vegetables in their own little garden, each child having his or her own plot to tend.

Maddie, at eleven was the oldest of this group, so he had shown her how to make oatmeal in the morning to feed all the children and soups and stews for lunch and dinner. She became their official cook, and seemed to enjoy creating new flavors with the onions and the bottled spices he brought home for her. Sometimes they cooked together if he was trying a new recipe. When Maddie asked if they could make a cake, he picked up the ingredients for cake and frosting on his next trip into Baraboo.

The man was not a naturally cruel person. When conflicts arose among the children in the basement or out in the backyard, he would take the perceived troublemakers up to the first floor of the house, set them down at the kitchen table, shoo the other children from the room, and have a quiet chat. Using the names that he had assigned to them, he reminded them that, right now, there was nowhere for them to go, that it was in their best interest to get along so that they could continue to come up to his rooms on first floor and do their assigned tasks. Otherwise they'd have to stay in the basement all the time, and maybe not even be allowed to play in the backyard. When the little troublemakers promised to be good, he'd give them some crackers and milk and send them on their way. It always worked. The kids all liked him and wanted to please him.

It wasn't difficult to keep the names straight. In any given batch, the first child taken was given the same name as the first child in all the other batches. The second children taken all shared the same name and so on. The only exceptions were slight alterations for boy versus girl, Marvin for Mary, for example. Also, if a teenage girl wasn't a virgin and seemed suitable for his own sexual pleasure, he'd give this special child an original name so that he could fantasize about her after she had been delivered.

With twelve, and soon to be fourteen youngsters in his house, the man knew that it was time to haul them to the LaCrosse warehouse. The basement was becoming too crowded. This would be his last load of children, and it would bring him a fortune. The man was almost a millionaire already; this final payment would put him over the top. At fifty-two, it was time to retire and move to a warm climate. He had already chosen the place where he would go and had begun moving his money to several local banks there, little by little so that nothing would seem suspicious, as he was using his real name. Ahhh, the man was careful, and smart, and clever. He would not be caught. Once retired, he planned to live an exemplary life, conforming to all of society's laws and expectations. He would be the good boy that his mother had always wanted him to be. He might even find a part-time job to blend in better with the people of the community.

Even as the man daydreamed about his future plans, he felt another urge growing inside him. Strangely, he could go for weeks and even months without thinking about sex. It just didn't seem important most of the time. An occasional jack-off in the bathroom off his bedroom was enough to satisfy him. But when the feeling in his loins began lightly, slowly building itself into his consciousness, he knew that his need was serious, unrelenting, until satisfied. He needed a woman.

The tall, easy-going man munched his sandwich and apple as he drove toward the secluded place where he had discovered teenagers making out and even having sex if the boys were lucky. There were never more than one or two cars there at the most; he had watched it from time to time. The older teens and twenty-year-olds used the spot later in the evening or even during the night. Younger teens seemed to use it after school or early evening, probably before their parents became suspicious of their activities. No fifteen or sixteen-year-old wanted their mother or father to find out that they were into heavy petting and oral sex, or even copulation. How embarrassing. He chuckled.

There were still a few hours before any teens would show up. The man found the secluded spot, drove a short distance beyond it, and backed the pickup truck out of sight among some trees. He had to push some branches aside to open the driver's side door and step out of the truck. Taking a couple of bottles of warm Orange Crush, he walked to the back of the pickup and untied the tarp.

First the boy. He pulled the frightened child from the truck, pulled part of the tape from his mouth, and removed the cap from the bottle. "Drink," he said, tipping the bottle up just far enough so the boy could suck liquid into his mouth. The child was thirsty. The man patiently allowed the little boy to drink a little at a time until the soda drink was gone. Then he re-taped the mouth and pulled the boy's pants down far enough to expose his penis. "We've got a long ride ahead of us," he said, "and there won't be any more potty breaks. You'd better pee now." The man held the tiny penis outward so the urine wouldn't wet the trousers. The boy let go with a stream that didn't seem to want to stop. He looked up at the man as the last few drops fell. "Good boy," said the man. "Lay quietly now, and take a nap." He lifted the child back onto the mattress, and pulled the little girl out.

She was as thirsty as her brother had been. The two looked enough alike to be twins, but clearly she was older. "How old are you, Sweetheart?" he asked. She didn't answer. "You must be about five. Is that right?" She nodded, leaning toward the bottle wanting another drink. He let her finish the bottle, and fastened the tape on her mouth once again. The man quietly explained that she had to pee now, because it would be awhile before they would stop again. "I have to take off your shoes and socks first and then your pants and underwear. Don't worry. It's only so that your clothes don't get soiled."

He pulled off her shoes and socks and left them by the truck. Then he guided her to a small flat area under a nearby tree, pulled the tape from her ankles and slipped her pants and underwear off. "Go ahead and pee," he said, supporting her as she squatted down. After a moment, she let go with both bladder and bowels, and began to cry. When she finished, he pulled her into a standing position leaning her against the tree for support while he pulled some fresh green leaves from the tree to clean her off. He walked her back to the truck, dressed her, and retaped her ankles together before placing her back on the mattress next to her brother.

He put the plastic tarp loosely over the children, but did not fasten it down. If he got lucky, another one would be joining them in a couple of hours.

This next one would be the crown jewel, the last one that he would ever take, and the one that would give him more pleasure than any that he had ever taken before. For her, he would delay delivery, so that she would become accustomed to him, so that she would trust him, so that she would desire him, and want him beside her every night. He would call her Vivienne, and she would want to be beautiful just for him. He felt himself becoming aroused, but not yet, not yet. He touched himself and pushed it down.

The children were quiet under the tarp. He had let their heads be partially uncovered so that they could breathe more easily. He dozed. How long he was asleep, he wasn't sure, but he awakened fully when he heard a car pull into the secluded spot just on the other side of the trees. The sun was low on the horizon and would soon drop out of sight over the nearby hills to the west giving a needed deep shade yet enough light for him to see what he was doing.

He didn't move. He wanted complete silence from where the truck stood. The only sounds were crickets and occasional bird calls. A dragonfly buzzed his windshield and flew off. He watched it lazily. He'd give the couple in the car a half hour to really get into it, clothes partially off, down on the seat, or maybe even having moved into the back seat, hands exploring, mouths sucking. They would be oblivious to his footsteps as he approached.

The man quietly turned the handle of the driver's side door, opened it slowly and slipped past the branches without making a sound. Oh, he was so good, so skilled. As he padded softly away from the trees and into the secluded area, he could see movement through the windows of the car. They were still in the front seat of the two-door sedan. He approached from the rear of the car, grabbed the door handle of the driver's side and yanked it open.

“Step outside, sir,” he ordered quietly.

The young man looked up. “What? What? Who are you? We haven’t done anything wrong.”

“Slide over to this side, and step out of the car!” the man said just a little louder, his voice demonstrating that he expected to be obeyed. The teenager got out of the car fumbling with his zipper.

“Lean over the hood of the car, stretch your arms out.” The boy did as he was told. The man quickly bound his ankles with tape.

“What are you doing? Who are you?”

The man did not answer. He shoved the boy hard to the ground stunning him. Before the teen could recover, the man flipped him onto his stomach, pinned him down with a knee on the small of his back, pulled the boy’s arms behind him and wound tape tightly around his wrists.

While the boy writhed and shouted, the man swiftly walked to the other side of the car and pulled out the girl who was still pulling up her panties. Speed and experience were all on the man’s side. He knew exactly what to do. He laughed aloud as she struggled against him. She was no match for his strength. In no time at all, her hands were bound behind her, her mouth was taped, and they were walking through the trees toward the pickup, away from the shouting boy.

The girl tried to run away as he reached to pull the tarp aside, but he had only to reach out and grab her once again. He set her gently on the ground and taped her ankles. When he pulled her to her feet, he could see her astonishment and utter terror upon seeing two small children tied up on a dirty mattress in the back of his pickup truck.

"You'll have a little company on the ride," he said hoisting her onto the mattress. The little ones began crying. "It's alright, darlings," he crooned. "We'll be home in just a few hours. Then you can meet your new brothers and sisters." He fastened the tarp tightly over the three of them, got into the cab, and pulled out onto the gravel road. He drove in the opposite direction from the secluded place where, presumably, the boy was still rolling around on the ground. It would take the man an extra half hour to go this way, but he didn't want the boy to see the pickup and be able to describe it to anyone later. The man smiled. Mission accomplished. He speeded up. All he wanted now was to get on home with his cargo, and tomorrow, after a good night's sleep, he'd begin priming his beautiful Vivienne to want him totally, insatiably, even shivering with desire.

It was well past midnight when the dogs came bounding to greet him as he drove up the long drive to his secluded home in the hills near Baraboo, Wisconsin. They made so much noise barking that surely all the children in the basement which was filled almost to capacity with children would be awake by now. The children would be glad to see him. They worried when he left them for days at a time even though they had plenty of provisions and even a radio to listen to 'The Lone Ranger' and other programs in the afternoon if the static wasn't too bad.

The man greeted his dogs, petting them and scratching behind their ears. A couple of them jumped up to put their forepaws on the back of the pickup's flatbed to sniff at the cargo, eager to sample the smell of these new children. The dogs were always more excited when there was more than one child. "Come on. I'll give you some fresh food and water before I unload. That should settle you all down while I carry the kids inside." The man unlocked the front door, turning on the light as he entered. He heard the children calling up to him. He unlocked the door to the basement and yelled, "Maddie, come up here."

The girl Maddie padded barefoot up the stairs into the kitchen, blinking at the bright light. "I want you to cook up some oatmeal, enough for three kids. Two of them haven't eaten since this morning, and they'll all sleep better on a full stomach," he said.

"Three?" she asked incredulously.

"Yeah, two little and one older than you. Get started while I feed the dogs and bring the kids in." He went outside with special treats for his four dogs. They had the run of the yard and the forested hills all around the place, yet miraculously were always right there waiting for him when he came home. He would hate having to put them down when he left this place. Maybe he'd keep one of them as a companion on his trip south, Jenga perhaps; he was the least vicious, even sweet at times when away from his companions.

The dogs were busy eating when he unfastened the tarp and pulled the first child out. He set her on the ground and took all the tape off her mouth, wrists, and ankles. "Stand here," he said, "while I get your brother."

He took both children by the hand and led them into the kitchen. "Maddie, take them to the bathroom and then feed them at the kitchen table before you take them downstairs. The man went to the basement door and called down into the semi-darkness, "Bruce, double up some kids and clear a mattress. I've got two more that can sleep together on the same mattress. Make sure they get a blanket. They'll be down in a minute with Maddie."

The man took his time going back out to the truck. The dogs finished eating and followed him. He climbed up onto the flatbed of the pickup, pushing aside the tarp and sat down next to the girl. "Now here is what is going to happen," he said. "I am going to take all the tape off and let you sit up. I will help you jump down from the truck onto the ground. Do not try to run away. There is nowhere to run." He continued speaking in a soft, soothing tone. "We are way out in hill country many miles from the nearest neighbor. Nobody can hear you if you scream except me and all the children in the house, and you'll only upset us all. You don't want to do that.

"As long as you are beside me, the dogs will not attack you. Should you try to run away, they will attack and could possibly kill you. I would not want that to happen. Maddie is feeding the children who came with you, and will leave a bowl of oatmeal for you as well if you wish it. She'll take the children to the basement to sleep with all the rest. Since the basement now has fourteen children, it's a bit crowded, and there is no room for you. I will show you where you'll sleep tonight." The man gently pulled the taped from the girl, freeing her arms last of all.

He helped her from the truck, and they walked into the house together, his arm around her shoulder to protect her from the dogs sniffing her dress, her hands, and the back of her legs and buttocks. "Don't be afraid," said the man. "They won't hurt you as long as I am here."

He was tired. It had been a stressful few days; the risk of being seen was always with him. There was no fear of being caught. Who would chase him way out in the country where he operated his business of taking children whom he found alone with no one to protect them. There was no law enforcement out there except for after the fact. The only person that he had ever allowed to see his face was the teenage boy probably still on the ground at a place so secluded that he'd wouldn't be found until the next romance-minded couple happened along. Didn't matter anyway.

He had enough money to buy an enclosed van in another town far from here where he wasn't known. After loading the children, he'd kill three of the dogs, toss their bodies in the kitchen, and set fire to the entire place. He'd leave no trace of what had once existed here. It had been the perfect setup for almost fifteen years of running this business, but it wasn't needed anymore. He would never return. He could thank that jerk he met in a tavern many years ago for steering him into this lucrative business; he still spotted him once in a while, but never acknowledged him. It was a wonder that the idiot hadn't been caught as he was sloppy and stupid, and delivered the kids one at a time as soon as he caught one. "He doesn't know my real name," muttered the man. "He won't be able to rat me out." The man would use this next week or two to tidy up his affairs and enjoy his Vivienne.

Maddie was just finishing washing the two bowls and glasses that the children had eaten and drunk from as the man guided Vivienne into the kitchen.

"Maddie, this is Vivienne. She'll sleep up here. You can get acquainted in the morning and we'll assign her chores then. A lot of the kids' clothes need mending. I'll get out the sewing basket and you can gather the clothing together for her to work on. "Go on downstairs now and put the kids to bed. Sleep tight, darling." He gave Maddie a kiss on the cheek and patted her shoulder. "You're a good girl," he said.

"Vivienne, there's some oatmeal for you, if you're hungry. Maddie made it just now." He pointed to the table and pulled out a chair for her to sit on.

"My name isn't Vivienne," she said.

The man gave a short laugh. "Listen my beautiful pet. From now on, you shall be called Vivienne. Any name you had before no longer exists. Any family you had before is now gone. We are your family now, at least for the time being, me, the kids downstairs who are your new brothers and sisters, and even the dogs that guard all of us from any intruders." He paused. "You'll like Maddie. She's been here the longest and knows the routine the best. She will show you how our family functions and you will fit in just fine.

"I know you're exhausted, Sweetheart. Sudden change is hard for anyone. Eat your supper while I wash up and get ready for bed." He left the room. When he returned a half hour later, he found Vivienne asleep with her head resting on her arms on the table, the oatmeal untouched.

The man gently lifted his lovely acquisition to her feet, led her into his bedroom and pulled the covers over her as she lay down. He pulled her shoes off and left her socks on. She lay still, not responding to his soft whispers. He was in his pajamas now and walked to the other side of his bed to crawl in beside her.

"Sleep well, my lovely Vivienne. In the morning we will begin your lessons when we both have our energy restored. You will come to like it very much. You will love what you are about to experience. Trust me," he said as he drifted into the land of dreams. "I will comfort you. It will be beautiful."

1

True Confessions

"Listen to this," said Alice, her face buried in the latest *True Confessions* magazine. She read, "She felt Brad move his hand from her shoulders and slowly down around her waist. Her heart was beating in anticipation. Would he continue his caress as he kissed her lips?'"

Silje had ridden her bicycle to town to meet Alice at her married sister Jane's house. Jane had stacks of *True Story* and *True Confessions* magazines that the girls loved to read. Silje knew her parents would not approve, but these were too good not to read. The magazines were filled with romance and the problems of women in love.

Silje giggled. "Listen to this one," she said. "'Judith turned her head very slightly casting her eyes to see if Corey was looking at her. If he was, she would know she was capturing his heart. Her heart sank. He was staring, not at her, but at her best friend Stephanie. Shocked, Judith stepped in front of Steph blocking Corey's sight of her. She was sure that Stephanie was not aware of Corey's interest, nevertheless, she felt herself growing angry. Corey was worth fighting for, even at the risk of losing her best friend.'"

"Yeah, I've read that one," said Alice. "Wait 'til you see how it turns out." She giggled.

"Sex? Do they have sex?"

"I'm not telling!"

Silje picked up a movie magazine and threw it at Alice. Laughing, Alice ducked, the magazine sailing over the sofa and falling behind it just as Jane entered the room. "Taking good care of my magazines?" she asked, setting down a tray of cookies and cola for the girls.

"Always," said Alice. "If we didn't take care of them, we wouldn't get to read them." She glanced at Silje and snickered.

"Thank you," said Silje, taking a drink of her cola. "I really appreciate your letting us hang out here sometimes."

"I like having you come," said Jane. When Ted is at work and I'm home all day alone, it gets a bit boring."

"Won't be boring when the baby comes!" said Alice.

"No, I can't wait. I'm tired of feeling like a blimp. Another couple of months, now. Ted wants a boy so he can teach him to hunt." Jane left the room.

"Do you suppose they still DO it?" whispered Silje.

"Ted probably stops only when he eats, sleeps, and goes to the bathroom," answered Alice, picking up a cookie. "He's always making remarks about it. Gets embarrassing."

"I suppose if you really like someone and they like you back, it must be tolerable. Lots of people do it."

"Maybe. Especially if the guy starts out slowly and works up to it. A girl might have time to figure out whether or not she wants to go that far."

"You know how I found out about sex? I was in the fourth grade at Homestead School and my best friend told me that my parents had sex and that's how I came into the world. I was horrified. Then she said, 'Yeah, they did it just like the bulls and the cows do it out in the pasture.' I didn't know what to say. I didn't want to seem like a dummy, so I didn't answer. I just let her talk."

"That is seriously gross!"

"I was so upset; I didn't want to play with her anymore. I did, of course, but I never forgot that conversation. That's why these magazines are so good. They show that girls have a choice in the matter too."

"I wonder what it will be like the first time."

"I wonder who it will be with the first time." Silje told Alice about the walk in the park with Freddie last year.

"Did you ever have sex with Charlie?"

"No, of course not. It was just kissing and talking. He never tried to go further. Charlie was a jerk though. We wrote letters to each other a few times. I kept them private and never showed them to anyone, but once when I was at his house, I found the letters I had written to him scattered around in his little sister's room. It really made me mad. His whole family had probably read them!"

"What did you do?"

"I pretended that I hadn't noticed, and when nobody was looking, I snuck into her room and stuffed all of them into my purse. He never said anything about it and I didn't mention it either. I broke up with him soon after. Jerk!"

"Yeah, you really have to be careful around boys. They are definitely not like us. I haven't gone out with anybody yet." Alice paused. "Someone has asked a few times, but I haven't said yes."

"Who?"

"Harry Olson."

"Oh, I know who he is. I've seen him in town sometimes on Friday nights. How do you know him?"

"He lives near LaFarge, not far from our farm."

"He's a good-looking guy. Why haven't you gone out with him?"

"He's nice, and I like him, but he has a brother that I'm not sure that I like."

"I've seen him. He seems quiet and pleasant enough. I wouldn't worry about him. If Harry is okay, and his family is nice to you, why not give it a try. It's only a date after all. You can always decline the next time if you didn't have fun the first time. And you might even like it."

The girls were done reading magazines and had eaten all the cookies and finished their drinks. "We're leaving, Jane. Thanks a lot!" they called.

Silje and Alice mounted their bicycles and rode side by side until they split apart, each riding to their own homes.

"See you, Monday!"

"One-and-a-half weeks to go!"

"Yayyyyy!"

16

Got Him!

Sheriff Joe Iverson had just hung up the phone talking with the principal at the Viroqua high school. The usual troublemakers had gotten into a fight in the school cafeteria again, all in fun of course, but a lot of spaghetti had ended up on faces and in hair. He'd send Otto over to the school tomorrow to have a talk with the offenders.

Iverson heard heavy footsteps coming up the stairs just before the door to his office swung open.

"Got him!" said Otto Bakke. Deputy Sheriff Bakke had just returned from following up a complaint of burglary in Stoddard, a small town in northwest Vernon County.

"Got who?" asked Iverson, looking up from the usual paperwork cluttering his desk.

"The kidnaper. He was scouting kids while the grade school in Stoddard was letting out for the day."

"How do you know it was him?

"Not much doubt," answered Otto. After finishing processing the grocer's complaint, I thought I'd drive around town a little before coming back. I spotted an old Plymouth coupe like Tom Galstad had described and then I saw him. The trunk of the coupe was half open, and this guy was standing behind a bush next to the car not doing anything, just standing there watching a couple of kids walking toward him."

"How did you get him?"

"I watched him for a couple of minutes to see what he was going to do. He let the two kids go past and waited for a lone child, a little girl to approach. She was dawdling along, picking up leaves and paying no attention to what was around her.

"This guy was so focused on the child that he didn't hear me come up behind him. Just as he stepped out on the sidewalk to grab her, I asked him what he was doing."

Otto laughed. "He saw my badge and tried to run, but I was ready for that. He didn't get very far!"

"Where is he now?"

"Down in the cell. I released Albert and locked Myron Larson up. Albert was pretty much recovered from last night's drunken rampage. Want to see Larson?"

"No. I'm tired. Let him stew overnight. I'll order a light meal for him from the restaurant. We can question him in the morning. Let's go home."

The next day, after briefing Otto on the situation at the high school, Sheriff Iverson called the principal and asked him to gather together yesterday's cafeteria hoodlums and provide a separate room for each of them to be interviewed one by one. "Otto Bakke will be over in about a half hour."

The sheriff descended the two flights of stairs and unlocked the door to the jail room. He flicked on the lights, just as Larson leaped to his feet from the cell cot.

"I don't know why I'm here." Larson whined. "I didn't do anything. You have to let me out."

Iverson ignored Larson and attended to some items on the table in the middle of the room. The contents of Larson's pockets were there including his wallet and his belt. Iverson had read Otto's brief report, so he already knew Larson's name and address. He turned to face the cell.

"I'm going to lock the door to this room and take you out of the cell. There is a telephone on the wall over there, and you may make one phone call. Then you and I are going to have a chat about your activities."

Larson was visibly nervous as he walked to the phone and dialed zero. He asked the operator to connect him to a number in the Sparta telephone exchange. "Henry, this is Myron Larson. I'm in jail in Viroqua. Can you get a message to my wife to call the sheriff here?" After a pause where Henry was obviously asking questions and Myron Larson was trying hard not to answer them, Larson accepted a slip of paper from the sheriff and read the phone number to the man on the other end of the line. After he hung up, he looked uncertainly at the sheriff.

"Sit down," said the sheriff quietly.

Barely able to control his shaking, Larson crossed the sizeable room and sat down at the table facing a wall with a couple of tall hand-built metal cells collapsed against it. Two cots were folded up nearby. Sheriff Iverson had scooped Larson's effects into a box, written his name and yesterday's date on it, and placed it on a counter next to the outer door.

The sheriff sat down on the opposite side of the table and watched Larson.

"Why was I arrested? I didn't do anything. I need to go home. My wife doesn't know where I am. My kids can't handle the farm without me." Larson pushed the chair away from the table and began to stand up.

"Sit down. You're not going anywhere. What were you doing in Stoddard?"

Larson sat down, his eyes shifting away from the sheriff's steady gaze. "Nothing. I mean I went there to buy some tools." His voice faltered.

"What tools?"

"I don't know. Just some things to fix my tractor. It's not running right now."

"Why were you watching the children walking home from school?"

"I wasn't. I wasn't!"

"Why did your car have the trunk lid half open? You were going to grab the little girl and throw her into it, weren't you."

"No, no. I was going to close the lid. That's why I jumped out on the sidewalk. That's what I was doing. I didn't even notice the girl. I didn't!"

The telephone on the wall rang, and the sheriff casually got up and walk to the phone to answer it. "Yes, he's here. Just a moment." He motioned Larson to come to the phone. "It's for you," he said.

Larson said hello into the mouthpiece and after that could barely say a word as a woman's voice on the other end yelled at him so loudly that the sheriff, leaning on the table could almost understand the words coming out of her mouth.

"No, no, I don't know when I'll be home. Soon. Soon. I haven't done anything wrong. They can't hold me here. The boys will have to do the milking until I get home." Pause. "Don't worry. I'll be back as soon as I get my car." More yelling.

"I had to leave my car when they brought me to Viroqua, but I'll get it back. I'll see you soon, soon. Bye."

Sheriff Iverson motioned Larson back to the table. "Sit down. Here is what is going to happen. I believe that you kidnaped six-year-old Archie Galstad more than a year ago, and were driving him into Trempealeau County."

"No! You're wrong. I didn't. I don't know anything about that!" Larson's voice had risen to a panic level.

"Archie was smarter than you, and he escaped. So we now have a witness who can identify you. Further, Archie's older brother saw you and your car, the very one parked on the street in Stoddard. He'll be able to identify the car, and possibly you also. We know it was you, Mr. Larson." Sheriff Iverson continued in the flat monotone that he had used throughout the interview, but now more firmly. His steely blue eyes gazed steadily at Larson's face.

Larson began to sob. "No, no. I didn't do anything. I just needed money. My farm doesn't bring in enough income to support a family, but I don't know about any kidnaping. I have kids of my own. I would never do something like that."

"We'll bring your car back to Viroqua and arrange a lineup of similar-looking men so that Archie and his brother can view you, and possibly identify you. In the meantime, we'll talk to the sheriff of Monroe County to see if there are any prior complaints against you. While we're up there, we'll pay a visit to your wife to see what she can tell us about your activities."

"She doesn't know anything. Leave her alone," said Larson, barely able to get the words out of his mouth.

"We'll be questioning you further about the kidnaping of children that's been going on throughout the State of Wisconsin in the past few years. Obviously you'll be able to tell us something about this as we already know that you operate in at least two counties."

Sheriff Iverson had been speaking in a firm impersonal monotone throughout the interview without changing his facial expression. He was aware of how disconcerting this technique could be to most criminal suspects, and Larson was no exception. By the time Iverson motioned Larson back into the cell, the man was trembling and could barely walk.

"You'll be given two meals each day, one in late morning and one in the late afternoon. Either I or Deputy Sheriff Otto Bakke will see you at least once a day, and you'll see someone from the restaurant delivering the meals. They have been instructed not to speak with you."

The sheriff turned the cell key locking Larson in, left the room and locked the outer door behind him. They had the kidnaper, Iverson was sure, but something nagged at him. Was he the only one? Who was he working with? Or for?

After a busy day tending to routine business, Iverson pulled into his driveway and saw his wife Marilyn give him a wave from the porch. He felt a flush of gratitude every time he saw her. A little on the stocky side, freckled, and rather plain looking, Marilyn was the best thing that had ever happened to him. She was not only a good mother to their young children, she could be trusted to repeat nothing that he told her about what was happening at work. He could tell her anything, and in return, he listened while she described her day.

Almost a decade ago, when he had asked a Westby farm woman, Emma Logan, to help solve the hay barn murder, Emma had decided that Joe Iverson needed a wife. She had the perfect candidate. During the trial of that long-ago killer, Emma managed to introduce Joe to her younger cousin Marilyn Logan. It wasn't difficult to get something going between them. Emma merely brought Marilyn with her to the trial each day and left her alone with Joe whenever she found an appropriate opportunity. Joe recognized Marilyn's quiet intelligence and empathy and began calling on her. It wasn't love at first sight, but the budding friendship showed Joe that here was the possibility of a wife that would be suitable for a local sheriff. Further, she was not from Vernon

County, but lived with her parents and siblings just outside of Rockbridge in Richland County, close enough to visit regularly, but out of his jurisdiction.

For Marilyn, moving to Viroqua worked perfectly. She was near enough to her cousins that Emma and her two brothers could keep the children when she and Joe wanted to have time alone, and also she was not far from her parents. She was happy. Joe Iverson, sheriff of Vernon County, was a dream come true.

Love grew.

Otto came upstairs from seeing Larson and reported that their prisoner was still defiant and angry.

"He'll have a different tune to sing after we get back from Sparta. The sheriff up there knows we're coming today. If we leave now, we should be back in early afternoon," replied Iverson.

While Otto drove, the two of them went over the details of the kidnapings and attempts at kidnaping in Vernon County. "We lost the girl down by Clockmaker School. That's the first one that we know of. She hasn't been found," said the sheriff.

"Then Archie, but he got away."

"Thank god," the sheriff muttered. "He and Tom will be the only witnesses who can identify Larson and the car. If we can get a confession out of this creep, then we'll have him nailed. He'll go to prison for a long time."

"Could be life," said Otto.

"Let's hope," said Iverson. "Then we've got Clara Mitby a year ago. We don't know for sure that she's not a runaway, but her parents are convinced she was taken."

"It's possible," said Otto, "although if she had someone, a boyfriend maybe, pick her up before the school bus arrived, the Mitbys wouldn't have seen that."

"They were pretty quick to move away from here. That was strange too. They were difficult people to get a handle on."

"I think that they were so strapped for cash that it overrode all other concerns, even the loss of a daughter. If you can't feed yourselves and your children, maybe it was a relief to move away and start over."

"Yeah, they never did seem to fit in. There was nobody here that they could turn to for help. No family."

"The neighbors were good about stepping up to help search for Clara though."

"A few did, but not like with Archie's disappearance. Alex Reiersen and the Logan brothers were really the only ones who made any real effort. Nevertheless, we've got to consider Clara

Mitby's disappearance as an unsolved case until she shows up. We'll grill Larson about her too."

The Monroe County sheriff had little to report about the Larson family. The Larsons could barely pay the taxes on the small plot of land that they owned, but no one in the family had ever been arrested. The oldest boy had been truant enough to get the sheriff's attention so he had warned Myron Larson to make sure that all his kids got to school. By law in Wisconsin, children had to attend until age sixteen, and Junior Larson had a year to go before he could officially drop out.

Otto drove into the hills outside of Sparta trying to follow the directions to Larson's farm that the local sheriff had given them.

"Wait. Back up. That's gotta be it, the road we just passed," said Iverson.

"That was a road?" laughed Otto, reversing the car and pulling off the gravel road onto a narrow dirt lane. In barely a minute they rounded a curve and saw a small farmhouse badly in need of paint. The barn and sheds nearby were tilting dangerously to one side. A woman and a small child came out on the porch and watched the two men in uniform exit their marked car.

As the men approached the house, the woman called out, "Where is my husband? What have you done to him?" The little girl, sucking on her thumb, clung to her mother's skirt as if the world was about to end.

"We'd like to talk with you about that," said Sheriff Iverson. "May we come in?"

"The porch is good enough," she answered. "There are some chairs here. Where is Myron?"

Otto sat down in an old painted rocker with no arms, but Iverson stood until the woman seated herself. Then he leaned against a porch column and began probing for information. "Your husband is fine for the moment. He's in a jail cell in Viroqua."

"What's he there for? What did he do? Not much probably. He's not capable of much of anything!"

Ignoring the woman's angry tone, Iverson watched her closely as he answered quietly. "Deputy Sheriff Bakke arrested him in Stoddard yesterday afternoon watching children leaving the grade school. He was about to grab a little girl walking by herself when Deputy Bakke intercepted him. Larson tried to run, but Deputy Bakke caught him."

The look of astonishment and dismay on Mrs. Larson's face seemed genuine. She hadn't known of her husband's activities. Recovering, she said, "No, you're wrong. He wouldn't do anything like that. I know him. You're mistaken." She looked past the sheriff at three children walking toward the house.

"What's going on Ma? What are they doing here? Where's Pa?"

"Molly, take the children inside. Junior, you stay out here." When the younger children were gone, Mrs. Larson said, "They've arrested your Pa."

"What? What for?"

"We believe that your father is involved in a kidnaping ring that has been operating throughout the state. We arrested him yesterday in Stoddard ready to grab a child and throw her in the trunk of his car."

"No. Pa's never done anything like that in his life. Ma, tell them."

"I did. They don't believe me."

"Mrs. Larson, we have two witnesses that we believe can identify your husband as the man who kidnaped a child in Westby a year ago. One of them is the child himself who later managed to escape. The car that the witnesses described matches the car your husband was using in Stoddard."

"We have a very strong case against him," added Otto.

"I would advise you to retain a lawyer to speak on his behalf," said the sheriff.

"Lawyer? Lawyer? We can't even pay the telephone bill. They took out our phone months ago," said Mrs. Larson.

"The car. Where is the car? We need that. It's the only way that we can get to town. The school bus won't come during the summer. We don't have horses anymore," Junior said, growing panic in his voice. "I work at a hardware store part-time. How will I get to work?"

"As soon as we can, we'll bring it back to you." said Iverson.

"When? How soon?" asked Junior.

"Probably in about a week." These people were the dirt-poor of Wisconsin's back woods, barely able to feed themselves off the land and making barely enough income to pay the taxes to retain their miserable plot of land. Or, like the Mitbys, unable to pay the rent wherever they were living.

As the men left, Mrs. Larson was sobbing openly. Her son put his arm around her shoulder, and they pulled open the screen door and went into the house. How could they tell the children that their father might not be coming home for a long long time?

"We'll have to get Larson's car tomorrow," said Iverson. "Maybe you can get one of the Logan brothers to go with you to bring it back."

"That shouldn't be a problem. I'll stop in at the high school around lunchtime to visit the cafeteria, and maybe even stroll through the halls to let our presence be felt. We can go after that."

Otto paused. "Myron Larson's wife has a mess on her hands. I wonder how they'll get along."

"I wouldn't worry too much. I suspect that she has been the strong one in that family for a long time. Those kids obey her, and the oldest one is already working in town."

"Yeah, Myron Larson doesn't seem especially bright. He's a weird little weasel."

"We'll get the car back to the family as soon as we can, and let them get on with whatever they have to do to rebuild their lives without that creep. They may find that they're better off without him," said Iverson.

"I can believe that!" answered Otto. "Maybe now, we won't see any more kidnaping attempts in Vernon County."

17

Mary Jane

Terror reigned throughout the county. Some parents were keeping their children home from school. It was almost the end of the school year anyway; they wouldn't miss much and would still pass to the next grade in the fall. Others in the countryside were arranging car pools to drive their children to and from school. The school buses still drove their regular routes but with fewer students riding. All students in Westby, Cashton, Viroqua, and other towns and villages had volunteer guards on street corners monitoring the students as they passed by, writing down their names to be sure that all who started out arrived at their destination.

The residents of Vernon County were shocked. Three children taken in one day! All were in the Coon Valley vicinity, and probably kidnaped by the same person or persons, but no one knew for sure. Speculation was rampant.

The first to be reported missing was Mary Jane Mason, a teenager who had been parked with her boyfriend at a grassy area just off a remote side road. The call had come in just as Sheriff Iverson was leaving the office for the day. Otto had already left.

"This is Sheriff Iverson."

"Hello, my name is Halfdan Dahlen. I need to report a kidnaping." The deep voice trembled uncertainly.

The sheriff was instantly alert. "Was someone in your family taken?"

"No. She's a high school student. She's my son's girlfriend."

"How do you know she was kidnaped?" False reports had tapered off, but this could be another one.

"Because my son was with her. The man tied Rich up and took Mary Jane."

"Is your son there with you? Let me speak with him."

The sheriff could hear muffled voices in the background before someone picked up the receiver and spoke into the mouthpiece. "Hello," a voice whispered.

"What's your name son?" asked the sheriff.

"Rich Dahlen," said the voice. "She was taken. A man took Mary Jane. . . ."

"All right. Tell me exactly what happened. Where did this take place? Was anyone else nearby?"

"No, nobody. We were parked by a road down near Coon Valley. We weren't doing anything, just sitting and talking."

"How long had you been there?"

"I don't know, a half hour maybe. This guy, this guy, pulled open the door and told me to get out. He sounded like a cop or something, so I did what I was told to do. I didn't know anything was wrong until I was leaning over the car with my hands and arms spread out on the hood.

"Before I could move he had tape around my ankles, and he pushed me to the ground. I tried to fight him but he was strong. He taped my wrists behind me and just left me there. Then, then. . . ." His voice broke.

"It's all right," said Iverson with more certainty than he felt. "We'll get to the bottom of this. What happened next? Where was Mary Jane?"

"She was still in the car. It all happened so fast! The man pulled her out of the car and taped her wrists and led her away into the woods. She tried to get away, but he caught her. She was calling for me, shouting my name. . . ." Rich broke down in deep uncontrolled sobbing.

"Let me talk to your father again," said the sheriff.

Halfdan Dahlen came back on the phone. "A farmer who lived on that road found Rich when he drove by. Rich had managed to move close enough to the road to be seen. He was still tied up."

"What time was this?"

"About five. We called you right away."

"Who is the young woman who was taken?"

"Her name is Mary Jane Mason. She's a junior in high school. Her family owns the farm next to ours. Rich and Mary Jane have known each other all their lives. They are very close friends."

Have her parents been notified?"

"No, I called you first."

"All right. I will come by and pick you up. We'll go together to talk with them. I don't think Rich should go with us at this point. Just you and me. By the way, what time was Mary Jane taken?" Halfdan Dahlen spoke with his son and came back on the line. "Rich picked her up when she got off the school bus at about three-thirty. It happened about a half hour later. That road just leads to some farms and doesn't go through to any other road so there's not much traffic on it. Rich lay there tied up for a long time." The sheriff got directions to the Dahlen farm, hung up and called Otto to let him know they'd had another kidnaping. As he hung up, the phone rang immediately. The operator at the central exchange had been holding the call until he got off the line.

"Sheriff, we can't find our children!" a voice shouted. "We've been looking all afternoon. They're gone!"

It was like all hell broke loose in the county. Word spread quickly that three more children were gone. Three! In one day! Taken AFTER Archie's kidnaper had been caught. What was going on? How many kidnapers were out there? Why was Vernon County being targeted? Why couldn't the sheriff stop this? Was he in on it? Nobody really knew him after all. He wasn't related to any of the major families in the county. He didn't grow up here. No one knew whether or not he was even a full-blooded Norwegian-American. And someone knew a cousin of somebody who had seen him in Coon Valley on the day the three latest children were taken.

As in so many insular communities of marginally educated older adults, rumors abounded, some began deliberately by people whom the sheriff had apprehended for various offenses however minor. Citizens of the county who had been helped by Iverson and Bakke tried to debunk the talk against the sheriff, but they were afraid of what was happening too. Someone was taking children. Whose kids would be next?

The sheriff and his deputy were working almost around the clock. They grabbed a few hours of sleep and a decent meal whenever they could get home to do so. Their wives knew to take over all family affairs that needed tending and kept the children quiet when their husbands were at home.

Sheriff Iverson contacted the state police and asked for assistance; he needed investigative help, clerical help, anything, but none was to be had. The State also was stretched thin with minimal budget to hire the personnel it needed.

"We're on our own," the sheriff told his deputy.

Iverson paid a call on Emma Logan and her brothers. "Emma, I really need your help, but it has to be more than the occasional ride-along to back one of us up while we interview possible witnesses. I'd like you to work full-time for the county, manning the sheriff's office, making calls, setting up appointments, and coordinating our investigations while Otto and I are out in the field. It's too much for the court secretary to handle and she doesn't have the training and know-how that you do."

Emma was silent for a moment, but her brother Boyd spoke up. "We've got a lot of the planting done, but there's a lot of work to do on the farm. It's summer, you know. Think we can handle it without her?" he said looking at his brother.

"Well," he drawled. "I suppose so, if you don't argue with me when I want to take a nap."

Emma smiled. "Looks like you've got a helper," she said. "When do you want me to start?"

"As soon as you can," answered the sheriff. "I'll get another desk in the office for you and a phone. It'll be crowded with three of us in the same room, but I'll see if we can get the judge to give us space in the storeroom next to us. They keep old records in it, and they could be moved to the basement."

"Can you afford a full-time helper?" asked Boyd bringing up the subject of money, always a delicate topic.

"We can't NOT afford it," answered Iverson. "I'll find the money somewhere in the budget, and you can be assured of being paid on time. Everyone wants these children found. There won't be any opposition to it."

"How about if I start on Monday?" asked Emma.

"How about tomorrow?" answered the sheriff.

Emma laughed without humor. "I'll be there at nine."

"Eight or sooner would be better," said the sheriff, grimly.

With Emma locating and talking with men who were potential candidates for the Larson lineup, Iverson began prepping Archie, Tom and their parents for what they would be experiencing. He wanted to be sure that Archie would be able to handle seeing his kidnaper once again. He was eight years old now and a bit mischievous, sometimes a bit too lively his mother said.

Sheriff Iverson also had asked a local lawyer to be present during the entire proceeding to ensure that later there would be no question as to the validity of the identification. It would be held in the jail room in the basement of the courthouse and in the corridor just outside the room that held Larson's cell. There was a window in the door to the jail room, and the Galstad brothers would view the lineup through the window. Larson and the men in the lineup would not be able to see the people in the corridor.

Emma had accepted men for the lineup only from Viroqua and villages to the south, men who had the same build and hair coloring as Myron Larson, and who would have been unlikely to ever have been seen by Archie or Tom. Sheriff Iverson wanted Myron Larson to be put away for a very long time, and wanted to be sure that the identification process went smoothly.

Deputy Otto Bakke was in charge of setting the scenario in the courthouse basement for utmost efficiency and smoothness of process. In the meantime, both of them had to field other complaints: a missing cow, an altercation outside a Cashton tavern, car accidents, and domestic quarrels turned violent, all in addition to the investigation of the most recent kidnapings. The sheriff's office needed at least one more deputy and full-time office help. The county board and supervisor must see that. This was an inhuman load to put on only two law enforcement officers, but there was no time to think about that right now. If Iverson allowed himself to dwell on it, he'd let his anger take his mind away from the tasks at hand.

The men who had agreed to be in the lineup were given their instructions. Enter the courthouse by the back door and proceed directly into the basement where they would be shown into a room adjacent to the jail. They were to speak to no one, not even each other. A court officer would be with them at all times. At an appointed time they would be led into the jail, given placards with large printed numbers and were to range themselves in a line facing the door according to numbers one through eight. Number seven was reserved for the man in the cell. After the prisoner in the cell was brought out to join the line, the lights would be turned out.

Sheriff Iverson met the Galstads at the front door of the courthouse and led them downstairs to a waiting area. "We'll take Tom first," said the sheriff. "This shouldn't take too long. You've already seen the car and identified it as the vehicle driven by the man who took Archie. Now I want you to see whether you can recognize the man himself. If you are not sure, you must tell me."

Tom nodded.

The sheriff explained the lineup procedure, and asked, "Are you ready?"

"Yes," answered Tom, and the two headed down the darkened corridor and around the corner to see a man standing outside the jail room. The sheriff introduced the lawyer to Tom who nodded at him but said nothing.

"Face the window in the door." ordered the sheriff. When Tom was in place, the sheriff rapped twice on the door, and from within the room, they could hear Otto Bakke call out, "Number one, step forward." A bright flashlight shown on a man's face. "Turn left," ordered Bakke. "Turn right. Now step back." Bakke repeated the procedure with the next man and then the next until he finished the line.

"Did you see the man who took Archie?" asked the sheriff.

"Yes," answered Tom. "It's number seven."

"Are you sure?"

"Yes."

"How do you know? It's been awhile since you saw him."

"I know. It's him. He turned and looked at me when I was running toward the car. He shut the trunk with Archie in it and looked at me again before he jumped in the car and drove away. It's him."

"Good. Thank you Tom. I'll walk you back to the waiting room. Do not speak to your parents or to Archie. Do not give them any indication that you identified the kidnaper. Understand?"

Tom nodded.

Sheriff Iverson motioned Archie and his mother into the corridor as soon as Tom entered the room. As they walked down the hallway and rounded the corner toward the lawyer, the sheriff kept up a constant stream of subdued conversation with Archie and his mom to try and relieve any anxiety they might have.

After introductions and thanking the lawyer for participating, the sheriff pulled out a low stool and placed it in front of the window. Archie climbed onto the stool with bravado and faced the dark window. He turned back and smiled at his mother. The sheriff rapped twice on the door.

Immediately a flashlight turned on in the dark behind the glass, and Otto said, "Number one. Step forward" A man holding a sign with a large number "1" hand lettered on it stepped toward the light. The flashlight shown on his face as he turned left, then right, and then straightforward again. Bakke moved to the next man and repeated the procedure.

"Don't say anything until we've been through this with all eight men in the lineup. Then I'll ask you if you saw the man who kidnaped you."

"No problem," answered Archie. "This is easy."

"Number five, step forward. . . ." Otto continued in a monotone taking his time, making sure that the person behind the window got a good look at each man.

"Number six, step forward. Turn left. Turn right. Step back."

Without breaking his rhythm, Bakke called out, "Number seven, step forward. Turn left. . . ."

"That's him," Archie whispered, putting his hands forward to lean against the door. He looked around the dark corridor for his mother. "Mommy. That's the man who took me." Tears streamed down his face. "He chased me. . . Mommy."

As Otto Bakke finished processing number seven and went on to number eight, Sheriff Iverson lifted Archie from the stool and into his mother's arms feeling the dampness where Archie had wet his pants. He rapped sharply on the door, and turned to indicate that Mrs. Galstad and Archie should go with him back to the waiting area. As they were about to round the bend, they saw the hallway behind them light up dimly as the lights were turned on the in jail room and shone through the small window. Archie turned to look back. The lawyer was gone; the corridor was empty.

Sheriff Iverson led the Galstad family up two flights of stairs into his empty office. Emma had gone to wait in another room when she heard them coming. The Galstads had many questions about Larson, how he was caught, and who the men in the lineup were. Larson's name would soon be public knowledge as he awaited trial, but the names of the men participating in the lineup could not be revealed.

The sheriff warned the Galstads not to talk any further about the kidnaping or the upcoming trial. "If you hear anyone in Westby threatening to take any action against Larson or his family, you must let me know. I want nothing to jeopardize this trial. We want this man to be put in prison for what he did. Thank you for coming in today. Tom and Archie, you did very very well. You were very brave to face this man again."

Otto Bakke locked Larson in his cell and escorted the seven men out to the back parking lot. He thanked the men for their service and handed out patches reading "Vernon County Volunteer" that each of them could attach to a jacket or shirt if they wished. Emma had done an amazing job of finding men that not only looked like Larson, but hadn't known each other prior to today. Yet Otto was sure that some of them would head straight to a restaurant for coffee to talk together. No matter. Aside from laying eyes on the kidnaper, they knew no more now than they had when they arrived.

Iverson, Bakke, and Emma Logan talked briefly about the day's event, breathing a collective sigh of relief that it was over. After setting out their plans for tomorrow, Iverson said, "Let's all go home and get a good night's sleep if we can. Emma, tell the operator that if any calls come in for us, that she can tell them to call tomorrow."

"Emergencies?" she asked.

"Don't invite that. If anything is a real emergency, she'll put it through."

18

When the Bubble Comes

They were glad to be done. You could see it in their faces, in the way they walked. For them, it was over, four long years of high school. Silje, Alice and Caroline sat together on the balcony of the gymnasium watching the seniors parade down the aisle to the chairs set up just for them, listened to the speeches all full of hope and promise for the future, watched them march one by one to receive their diploma from the principal.

"I think I'm going to die . . . ," muttered Caroline.

"What's the matter?" asked Alice.

"Another whole year here. I can't take it!"

"We'll be seniors," whispered Silje. "We'll be the important ones. Look at it that way. We'll get through it somehow."

"Not much choice," giggled Alice.

"Maybe we'll get snatched and taken to a magical kingdom full of cute boys and lots of dancing," muttered Caroline.

Silje let out a spontaneous guffaw and quickly covered her mouth and tried to look innocent. Someone in the crowd below looked up toward the balcony, but couldn't identify the noisemaker. Then it was over. The graduates threw their caps in the air and the gym erupted into noise and confusion as graduates and families worked their way through the crowd trying to find one another.

Silje and her friends followed the balcony crowd down the stairs and out into the warm sunshine. None of the girls had attended the baccalaureate service held at the Lutheran church in Westby on Sunday night. There was space only for the graduates and two members of their families for this combined Catholic-Lutheran-Methodist worship service commemorating and sending forth this year's class of high school graduates into the world to do great things. The somber service was always held a few days before the graduation ceremony so as to capture the more serious and hopefully godly aspect of what these young people should be thinking about. In a year, it would be Silje dedicating her life to God.

The girls spotted Edwin and Freddie talking earnestly with a young man that they didn't recognize "What's up?" asked Caroline walking up to Edwin.

"Rich wants us to help look for Mary Jane," said Freddie.

"How are you going to do that?" asked Alice.

"Are you Mary Jane's boyfriend?" interjected Silje.

"Yeah, he is," said Freddie. "He's a cousin of Edwin's. He never went to high school. That's why we never met him. He lives way down by Coon Valley."

"Oh," said Silje, looking over the tall silent young man who couldn't seem to meet Silje's gaze. Rich looked nothing like Edwin. Much better looking, but that wouldn't take much.

"Tell them," said Edwin. "If they know, maybe they'll help us."

"Mary Jane is going to have a baby," Rich blurted out in an anguished voice, his normally stoic face almost breaking. "We have to find her. We have to bring her home."

So that's why she was throwing up in the bathroom. She's pregnant. Oh my gosh! Mary Jane and Rich have been having sex!

Silje looked toward Alice. She could tell that Alice was thinking the same thing that she was: romance magazine stories come to life!

"I don't see how we can help," said Caroline. "I would if I could, but where would we look? She might not even be in the county anymore. The man could have taken her anywhere."

"She's a prisoner. I know she is. If she could come home, I know she would." Rich's voice strangled.

Edwin moved closer to his older cousin. "Listen Cuz. We'll help. If you have any ideas of where we might look, just tell me. I'll get some of us together, and we'll go there. We'll knock on doors, anything."

Rich nodded, turned, and walked away.

It was futile, of course. Rich didn't call, and summer activities began immediately to take their attention. Farm kids were busy helping their parents tending crops and domestic animals. Who knew how the town kids spent their time?

The June wedding dances started up in Cashton's community hall—two and sometimes three a week.

George, Caroline's brother, made the rounds picking up Caroline's girlfriends to give them a ride to the dances. Silje, Alice, and sometimes one or two others crammed themselves into George's small car. Lutheran and Methodist brides and grooms were not permitted to hold wedding dances if they wanted to married in their respective churches, but for Catholics, it was tradition, a part of the wedding day and evening ceremonies. The wedding dances were public events and anybody could come whether or not they were acquainted with the bride or groom: men, women, grandpas, grandmas, children, and above all, teenagers out to have a good time. Chairs lined the sides of the dance hall and up in the balcony where people could go to rest or to watch the dancers.

The um-pah-pah of the tuba set the beat for the guitar, accordion, drums, clarinet, and sometimes a piano. When a fiddle or a banjo was part of the band, the dancers were in heaven. Beer Barrel Polka, The Danube Waltz, fox trots, and the occasional schottische for threesomes provided the pulsing rhythm that shook the community hall and let everyone within blocks outside know that a good time was being had inside.

Silje was a good dancer, and was a popular partner. She had taught herself to feel the rhythm of the beat and the dancing style of her partner. She could follow the dance steps of almost anyone, and was rarely left on the sidelines to watch others. Now she was growing tired and needed to rest. She pushed her way through the crowd at the back of the hall and made her way to the narrow basement stairs.

"Hi," she said to Edwin's younger sister Marjorie who was coming up the stairs. Silje knew Edwin's family only by sight, but she ventured the question anyway. "Has Edwin heard from Rich yet?"

"No," answered Marjorie, looking away and pushing past Silje. "We don't know anything."

"Oh, okay." Silje continued down to the tiny foyer on the lower level and pushed on the door to the ladies' room. It was miraculously empty. There were two stalls and a single badly chipped sink. She entered the stall furthest from the sink, closed the door, and pulled out some toilet paper to wipe off the seat just in case there was moisture on it from the previous user. She sat down, relishing the quiet. She heard someone enter, use the other toilet, and leave without washing her hands. Silje pulled up her panties, lowered the lid, and continued to sit inside the stall. Women and girls came and went using the remaining toilet; no one questioned who was in the closed stall.

In spite of the pounding beat of the music upstairs and the coming and going of women into and out of the restroom, Silje's mind seemed to stop, to empty. She was dimly aware that the bubble was present again, the feeling that she was looking at her surroundings through a transparent barrier, like looking through a glass window, like being in a bubble apart from the world around her. It had been coming more frequently lately, and when it was present, it seemed as if the bubble had always been there, but maybe not. When she was with her friends, she didn't think about it. Maybe it wasn't there then, but suddenly, especially when she was alone, or even in the presence of other people with whom she wasn't talking at the moment, the bubble would appear, and she would become intentionally aware of having to look through it to see what she assumed was the real world around her. Sometimes she just let it have its own existence, let it be, and retreated into herself, watching her thoughts rather than her surroundings. A feeling of deep sorrow sometimes descended upon during these times. She had never tried to fight the barrier; it was easier to let it be and wait until it disappeared on its own. While it was present, it seemed that her conscious mind was trying to sort itself out a bit.

Where are they? Clara has been gone so long now that practically everyone has forgotten her. I haven't. Clara, if you ever come back, I swear I'll be more kind, more your friend than I was before. God, please, please, bring Clara back. I'll be her best friend. I promise, God. I want to do it all over.

Silje remembered the time at Homestead School when she hated Clara and her bossy mocking personality so much that she had plotted various ways to cause her death and eliminate her once and for all. She had worked out various schemes in her mind, but none would work without her being discovered as the perpetrator. Then it had dawned her how such an act on her part would hurt her parents, and the scheming began to recede. Silje resigned herself to putting up with Clara and to avoid her as much as she could, and that had become their so-called relationship in high school.

I'm sorry, God, really I am. I'll never hate anyone ever again. I promise. Hating doesn't work anyway. It doesn't do anyone any good, especially the hater. Especially me.

Her thoughts wandered. She leaned forward, put her elbows on her knees and stared at the floor. The door to the restroom opened. Silje heard Alice and Caroline enter busily chatting. "Who's taking you home? asked Alice as she entered the second stall.

"Don't know yet. I'm hoping one of the twins will ask me."

"Oh, I beat you to it!" called Silje from behind the stall door. "One of them asked me."

"What are you doing in there?" asked Alice.

"What do you suppose I was doing?" said Silje emerging from the stall. "None of your business, that's what!" The girls all laughed, washed their hands and headed out of the ladies' room and up the stairs.

"Really? One of the twins asked to take you home? Which one?" asked Caroline.

"The shorter one. The one who had rheumatic fever when he was little."

"The taller one is cuter," said Caroline. "Maybe I can get him to dance with me."

"You can hardly tell them apart," said Alice. "Only when they stand next to each other, you can see that one is taller."

"And straighter," said Caroline. "Anyway, I'd take either one. They are tall, handsome, blonde, and so very Norwegian-looking. How did you manage to get asked?"

"I don't know. He asked me to dance twice and then asked me. His brother will probably be in the same car with whomever he asks to take home. I'd better get back out and connect with him."

"Lucky you," said Caroline.

"I think I need to find George and ask if I can ride home with him," said Alice. "If Harry were here, I know he'd ask me."

"Yeah, the dance is almost over. We'd better find our rides."

After the final slow waltz that signaled the end of the dance, Billy took Silje's hand and led her out of the hall and to an old gray Ford parked a couple of blocks away. The streets were full of people streaming out of the community hall to go home or back to the taverns which would be open for another hour until one o'clock.

Silje noticed a slight beer-breath from Billy when he leaned over to kiss her as he opened the car door and pulled the front seat forward so that she could enter the back. Close behind, came Billy's brother Barry with a girl that Silje had never met.

"Where to?" asked Barry starting the engine.

"Head toward Westby, and I'll tell you where to turn off," answered Silje. "I live right along the highway. It's about six miles from Cashton."

"Will do. That's not bad. My brother once asked a girl who lived so far out in the country that we couldn't find our way back!"

"Ignore him," said Billy putting his arm around Silje and pulling her closer. She rested her head on his shoulder. The two in the front seat were already deep into a prolonged kiss and probably early fondling. They broke apart, and Barry started the engine. The car pulled out of its parking spot and drove out of town toward the highway to Westby.

Silje turned toward Billy to say something, but the thought was lost as he leaned down and kissed her softly, pulled away, looked at her briefly, and then leaned in for another one. Silje quickly ran her tongue over her lips to moisten them again before she felt the growing pressure of Billy's lips upon hers.

Far too soon, she glanced up to see that the car was almost at the driveway to the farm. "Next one," she called out to Barry. "Turn left at the next driveway."

The old car rumbled up, over the railroad tracks, down the curve toward the farm buildings, and came to a stop in front of the house. Turning off the engine, Barry got out and pulled the back of the driver's seat forward to let Silje and Billy out.

"This was nice," said Billy. "Maybe I'll see you at another dance soon."

"Okay," answered Silje. "I come pretty often, so I'm sure we'll run into each other."

One last kiss and the evening was over. Silje watched Billy walk back to the car and climb into the back seat. Barry turned the car around and drove away.

Wow, I got a ride home with one of the blonde twins! Can't wait to tell Alice and Caroline all about it.

Silje was sure that Billy wasn't boyfriend material. They lived too far apart for one thing—although Charlie had lived on the other side of Cashton too, and he used to come to take her out.

Still it was different with Billy. He was cute and handsome and nice, but there hadn't been any real connection between them, no special attraction.

It's enough to have gotten asked by this gorgeous Norwegian god. I was noticed! He asked ME! Oh my gosh!

Silje tip-toed through the kitchen, through the tiny living room and into her bedroom. Stripping off her skirt, blouse, and underwear, she crawled into bed.

"You home?" Silje's mother muttered from the other bedroom.

"I'm home," she answered, turning toward the wall, pulling the sheet and blanket up around her ears, leaving only her nose exposed so that she could breathe.

She fell asleep quickly, maybe to dream, maybe not.

19

Silje Expands Her World

Every Saturday for the past two months, Silje had taken the Greyhound bus to LaCrosse to receive eye treatments. She would wait in front of Unseth drug store on Main Street in Westby for the bus to stop on its way from Madison to LaCrosse. Dr. Ore, the ophthalmologist had told her mother that Silje would benefit from eye exercises before he updated her prescription for new glasses, so Silje dutifully rode the bus to LaCrosse, arriving at the bus station at eleven, walked through stores until she knew them all by heart, ate a hot dog at the Coney Island hole-in-a-wall restaurant, and got to the eye doctor for her one o'clock appointment. For half an hour, Silje sat in a dark room moving her eyes up, down, left, right, following a red light in a machine until the doctor released her. *Boring, boring, boring.*

Today, her mother had given her money for a movie, and there was just time enough to see "Ivanhoe" with her idol Elizabeth Taylor before catching the four o'clock bus back to Westby. *I wish I looked like her.*

She bought a ticket, got a small bag of popcorn, and entered the almost-empty darkened theater where previews were just beginning. Her English class, last year, had studied the book and Silje hadn't understood it very well. Maybe the movie would be better than the book had been; anyway, anything with Elizabeth Taylor was bound to be exciting. *Maybe if I dyed my hair black.*

Silje chose an empty row near the back and moved past five empty seats to settle into the seat next to the wall. The previews were almost over when a man entered her row. He slowly bypassed four empty seats to slip into the one next to her. Silje became immediately wary. Why would someone choose that seat when the theater was practically empty? Nevertheless, she was trapped, and couldn't move away from the man, so she ignored him, leaned closer toward the wall and continued to munch her popcorn while waiting for the movie to begin.

Just as the opening credits for "Ivanhoe" were scrolling across the screen, Silje felt the man reach his right arm across the back of her chair and lower it toward her shoulders. Simultaneously, his left hand touched her knee and began to slide upward.

"What are you doing?" yelled Silje, jumping to her feet as she shoved the man away. As she kicked at his legs, the popcorn spilled all over him, and he leaped to his feet and fled. Stunned at what had just happened, Silje watched the man run up the aisle and out into the lobby. The other movie patrons turned to see what the commotion was, but it had happened so fast that there was nothing left to see. They turned back to watch the beginning of the movie.

Silje stood for just a moment and then walked toward the aisle. The bag of popcorn still had some left in it, and she had paid to see this movie, so she might as well stay to watch it. If the man was still in the lobby, she didn't want to encounter him if she left, and anyway he might follow her out to the street. If she left now, she'd still have hours before the bus to Westby arrived at the station.

By the flickering light of the movie screen, she could see three middle-aged women sitting together in the center section on the aisle. Silje slipped into the aisle seat in the row just in front of them and pushed herself down with her head against the back of the seat so as not to obstruct their view. *This ought to be safe.*

I learned a lesson today. Never, never put myself in a position where I could be trapped by someone, where I couldn't get away. If I go to the movies alone ever again, I'll always sit in an aisle seat.

After a few minutes her heart stopped beating so hard and her breathing settled down. She was safe now. Later, when the women walked out of the theater, she would follow right behind them and stick with them for a block or two to be sure that nobody was following her. Then she'd walk quickly to the bus station and buy her ticket back to Westby.

Silje had to concentrate on the story up on the screen to try and sort out who was on whose side in all the battles and political intrigue, but it was fun to watch Joan Fontaine and Elizabeth Taylor. In Silje's opinion, Ivanhoe should marry Rebecca instead of Rowena. She remembered the story's ending from English class. If this was what Sir Walter Raleigh called a happy ending, Silje could teach him a thing or two. Maybe she'd write her own stories someday.

One Saturday while meandering along the street in LaCrosse, Silje saw a sign "Help Wanted" in the window of Kreske's Dime Store. On impulse, she went in and asked about it. Before she knew what was happening, she was escorted to a small office on the balcony overlooking the sales area below and was staring at an application for a sales clerk position. Silje picked up the pen and filled it out. *Why not? I won't get it. They'd never hire me!*

Later, she casually mentioned it to her mother and father during supper that she had filled out an application just for fun and was surprised that her parents took it seriously.

"Well, I suppose you'll have to drive, then. The bus won't get you to work on time," said Alex.

"She can take the car, I suppose, but not every day. I need it sometimes too," said Pauline.

"I probably won't get the job," said Silje, alarmed that her parents were willing to let her work at a job in LaCrosse. She'd never had a paying job before. She wouldn't know what to do. What if she broke something? What if they didn't like her? They might fire her! She'd die if that happened!

"She can have the car on Monday, Tuesday, and Thursday," said Ma, ignoring Silje. "I need it on Wednesdays and Fridays."

Silje listened to her parents discussing her job application as if she'd already gotten the job. Her father used the Ford pickup truck most of the time, and only drove the Packard sedan when they were going somewhere as a family. Her mother had Ladies Aid on Wednesdays once a month and Church Circle on Fridays. She picked up Aunt Minnie and neighbor Julia Hoffman for the Ladies Aid meetings as neither of them could drive. Aunt Minnie depended on Pauline for

Church Circle too. It was complicated. *I don't know how Ma keeps it all straight.*

By the time supper was over and she was drying the dishes, Silje felt like the job was a done-deal, even though it hadn't even been offered to her. This was moving faster than she'd expected, and she was beginning to feel excited about working as a sales clerk. They had to give her the job; they had to. *I want to tell Alice and Caroline that I have a job. In the city! In Lacrosse. A real job that paid actual money! Oh my gosh! I'll be a working girl!*

On Sunday, Pauline and Alex decided to go to church, and, of course, Silje went with them. *Boring*. It was the usual—Silje stood around while her parents chatted with relatives and neighbors. Then they sat in uncomfortable wooden pews facing front while Pastor Martin led the hymn singing and gave a boring sermon. Silje felt that she owed it to God to listen to the preaching, but that lasted for about two minutes before her thoughts began to drift. She glanced at her parents. Ma was looking at her hands folded in her lap; Pa was dozing.

After the service was over, all the people walked up the aisle of North Coon Prairie Church and out into the sunshine. Some milled about, walking through the cemetery that surrounded the small country church, and others walked directly down the sidewalk, past the thick hedges and into the parking lot, got into their cars and went home. Thank goodness. To Silje, the services had seemed to last forever. She hadn't seen anybody of interest so she walked quickly to the car, got in and waited for her parents to chat their way to joining her.

When they got home, Silje hurried out of her dress and into a pair of shorts and her favorite plaid short-sleeved shirt. "I'll be in the tree!" she called to her mother as she dashed out the door. Ma would call her when Sunday noon dinner was ready. Silje climbed onto the lowest branch of the old gnarled apple tree and leaned back against the trunk, opened her book and buried herself in *The Clue of the Black Keys,* a Nancy Drew mystery that she'd purchased in LaCrosse yesterday. There hadn't been any dances last week, and books were her only salvation.

On Monday, at about two in the afternoon, Silje was picking ground cherries in the vegetable garden when Pauline appeared on the porch and yelled, "Silje! Silje! LaCrosse is on the phone."

Oh my gosh. Silje almost peed in her pants as she ran toward the house. They were calling! They were going to tell her that she didn't get the job. She tried to calm down as she walked past her mother and picked up the receiver on the telephone hanging on the wall near the stove.

"Hello . . . ?"

"Is this Silje Ry. . .Rier. . . ." a man's voice stumbled.

"Silje Reiersen, yes," said Silje.

"This is Manning Fox at Kreske's. I have an application from you for a sales job. Are you still interested?"

"Yes. Yes," said Silje.

"Can you be here at nine tomorrow morning?"

"Tomorrow is Tuesday. Yes, I can be there," Silje hesitated just a moment. "I can work on Mondays, Tuesdays, and Thursdays," she said. "Is that okay?"

"Well we were hoping that you could work a full six days," he said, but I have another applicant who also wants part time. I'm sure I can work the two of you around each other. Be here at nine tomorrow, so we can teach you the cash register. The store opens at ten."

"I'll be there," said Silje.

Manning Fox continued, "You'll work nine to five each day; the first hour is straightening the merchandise from the day before and stocking the counters. We'll assign you to a certain sales area in the store where you will familiarize yourself with all the items for sale, and then help customers to find what they want and wait on them as they buy. The job pays seventy-five cents an hour."

"Where can I park the car?" asked Silje.

"There is an alley behind the store. There are some spaces reserved for staff. You'll see a sign for which of the parking spaces belong to Kreske's. Okay?"

"Okay. I'll be there!"

Silje hung up the receiver and looked at her mother. "I got the job!" she whispered, her eyes wide.

Pauline laughed. "I'm sure you'll do just fine."

"I got the job! I got the job! I've gotta call Alice. I've gotta call Caroline. Oh my gosh! I'm a working girl!"

The summer of 1952 sped by. On three days a week, Silje drove to LaCrosse and worked at Kreske's Dime Store. She came home exhausted, but a little supper gave her the energy to go to the dances in Cashton or Ontario or even Reedsburg, or roller skating in Sparta, or to a movie in Westby with her friends. On Saturday, she continued to take the bus to LaCrosse to visit the eye doctor.

If these eye exercises are doing any good, I can't see it. I have to keep it up, though, so he'll give me better glasses for school this fall. Groan! At least I'm getting to know downtown LaCrosse. If I walk a different section each Saturday, I'll know it so well that I could make maps of it. Maybe I could sell my maps. And make more money. It's amazing how good money makes you feel.

Soon after Silje began working, Pauline had taken her to the bank in Westby and helped her set up a savings account so that she would learn how to manage money. Silje loved to watch the balance grow. The less she spent, the more she had in the bank. It was a miracle. Her take-home pay was eighteen dollars a week and at first, she put the whole amount in the bank. Then she realized that if she kept five dollars out, she wouldn't have to ask Ma for money anymore. She could be independent. Oh my gosh. Money of her own. Her very own.

Before she knew it, the calendar turned over into August, and school would begin again in just a few weeks.

16

Lost and Found

Where hadn't she explored yet? Wherever she went, it had to be within walking distance of the bus station; she didn't want to get stuck waiting for the eight p m. bus if she missed the four o'clock bus. Dr. Ore had measured her vision today, and Silje had picked out new frames. She'd get them next week, and then it was over. *No more Saturdays in LaCrosse; it was soooo boring.*

She had three more weeks of working at Kreske's Dime Store though. Ma was letting her work on Fridays too, so she was making a lot more money, but she had to admit it was tiring. *I'll be SO glad when school starts.*

Silje turned the corner and found herself on Third Street. It was dingy without any stores of interest, only small convenience stores, taverns, and creepy men milling about in twos and threes. They didn't pay any attention to her, but she walked quickly anyway. *Maybe this was a mistake. Maybe I shouldn't be here.*

After walking a couple of blocks, Silje decided that she'd rather just go back to the bus station and wait there. It was only an hour more until the bus came, and she could sit and read the movie magazine that she had purchased at the Doerflinger's Department Store book section. *If I cut through this alley to Fourth Street, I'll be almost there. It will be faster than going back and all the way around.*

Silje was not in any rush. The alley was long but empty. It was wide enough for delivery trucks to pass through, but this was Saturday afternoon, and no merchandise was being hauled in right now. She was alone. The noise of the minimal traffic on Third Street faded as she walked deeper into the alley. Her thoughts drifted.

I don't have a boyfriend right now. That's okay. Caroline doesn't either. Alice is getting closer to Harry and they go out sometimes, so she probably won't be available much next year. Tillie, from the school bus likes me, and maybe I'll pal around with her more even though she's a year behind me. We always have a good time walking down the hill together. Sometimes she saves me a seat on the bus in the afternoon, if she gets on before I do. I'll ride my bike to town while the weather is still nice, but on rainy days, or when the cold and snow come, I'll be back on the bus as usual.

The loading dock on her right was set back from the alley so that trucks could back into it and unload their merchandise. It was in shadows now and empty. *Spooky . . . probably full of Kleenix box spirits chasing toilet-paper ghosts trying to see who can hold the most snot.* The big iron doors at the back were closed with a padlock and a bolt lock above that. Silje increased her pace.

A smaller loading dock was just up ahead bordering directly on the alley. Trucks would have to unload while parked in the alley, but maybe the loads were smaller, or the trucks were quickly dropping off just a few items; it would have to block the alley while it unloaded.

Silje heard faint voices up ahead, men's voices and another sound sort of like kittens mewing. She saw nothing, so she continued walking. She could see occasional cars on Fourth Street way ahead of her; she hadn't realized that this alley was so long.

Suddenly, she walked into a hidden intersection: another alley to the right that seemed to run between the alley in which she was walking and another parallel alley to the east. A truck was parked about half way between the two major alleys. Silje hesitated, and then backed up to the corner that she had just passed. Carefully, she poked her head forward and watched, curious to see what the men were loading into the truck.

The back of the large truck was facing toward her, and Silje heard strange sounds from the cages being carried up the truck's ramp to be piled one upon another all the way to the ceiling of the truck's container. A couple of men stood inside the truck hoisting the cages up, as two or three, or maybe four, men hurriedly brought them out of the warehouse. Silje heard a faint scream that seemed to come from inside the warehouse.

What kind of animals are they hauling?

Some cages had a single large animal, some held two smaller ones. If one of the animals cried out, the men on the ground shook the cage and told it to shut up. Silje heard one of the men say that they should have been given a stronger dose.

Dose? Dose of what? What's going on?

A scream came from inside the ware-house, louder than before. *That was no animal. I know what animal screams sound like, pigs being butchered especially. That was a person, a human being, a woman! The scream came again.*

"Tell them to shut her up until we're gone. Then she can holler all she wants!"

Silje's jaw dropped. *Those aren't animals in the cages. Those are children!!* She could see little fingers clutching the cross-bars in a cage with only one child in it. "Please," she heard a girl's voice pleading."

"Quiet, or we'll give you another shot," ordered the man in the truck swinging the cage and dropping it roughly on top of another one. The truck was almost full.

Oh my gosh! Oh God! Those are the stolen children! They're alive. Captured. They're being taken somewhere.

"Hey!" yelled a male voice. "Someone's there! Kurt, is that you? Show yourself, damn it! Stupid kid. He's run off."

Footsteps approached the place where Silje had stood. She was afraid to cross the intersection to run toward Fourth Street, they might see her, so she turned and ran back the way she had come. She heard footsteps running behind her, but she didn't turn her head. She just ran, and ran as fast as she could. She saw nothing on either side of her, not the loading docks or anything else. She ran; it seemed like forever before she turned the corner onto Third Street and the running footsteps seemed to stop, but she couldn't be sure. She kept running, almost knocking down a staggering old man in her path. She ducked around him and kept running. Voices called out to her, "Where you going so fast, Chick-a-dee? Ain't nothin' that important! Slow down." She ignored them and kept running, past the taverns, past the dingy stores, and finally turned left onto a street leading back to Fourth Street.

She slowed to a fast walk, almost out of breath. By the time she climbed the steps into the ticket office at the bus station, she was breathing hard and felt almost faint.

There were only a few people in the wood-paneled waiting room in front of the ticket window, a very tired-looking mother with two small children napping beside her on the worn bench on which she sat, and a couple of teenage boys who didn't seem to know each other. A middle-aged man had entered just before Silje and was heading for the single glass window behind which a bored-looking ticket agent sat. Silje speeded up and cut in front of the man. "I'm sorry," she muttered, as she passed him.

"Please, you've got to help me," she leaned toward the glass and called through the round window to the ticket agent. "I need to call the sheriff in Viroqua. It's an emergency." The agent looked at her blankly. "Can you get him on the phone? Hurry!"

"What's the matter?" said the man behind her.

"I saw them!" said Silje, on the verge of tears. "The children, the missing children. They were loading them onto a truck. They were all in cages. I need to tell Sheriff Iverson! He'll know what to do."

The man leaned around Silje and shouted at the ticket agent. "Unlock the door, and let her in. Now! Or I'll break the glass and get the phone myself!" The man was big, and puffed up his shoulders as he leaned toward the window. Everyone in the waiting room was now on alert watching the menacing man and the young frightened teenage girl. The two children awoke crying.

"All right. All right, but just her, not you." The agent got up from his chair and unlocked the door to his office. He opened it just enough to allow Silje to slip through. "The phone's over there," he said indicating a narrow counter on the back wall. He re-locked the door.

Silje hurried across the small office, picked up the receiver, heard the dial tone, put her finger in the last circle on the wheel and spun it around.

"Operator," said a voice.

"Please get me the sheriff in Viroqua. I don't know the number. It's urgent! It's an emergency!"

"One moment please."

Be there. Please. Be there!

It seemed like minutes passed before Silje heard the ringing on the other end, and finally a woman's voice answered. "Sheriff's office. Emma speaking. May I help you?"

"I need to speak to Sheriff Iverson. Is he there?"

"Yes, who may I say is calling?"

"Silje Reiersen. Tell him I saw the missing children. I know where they are!"

Another phone was picked up immediately. "Silje, what's this about the missing children?"

"They're here. All of them. In LaCrosse. I saw them. They were in cages, and some men were loading them in the back of a big truck. They're in an alley down near Third Street." Silje caught her breath." *Believe me. Please believe me.*

"Silje, where are you now?"

"At the bus station in LaCrosse."

"I want you to stay right there. I'm calling the LaCrosse police. Wait until they show up, and go with them to the alley where you saw the children. Can you locate it again?"

"Yes, I think so."

"I'm leaving right away. I'll be there in about forty-five minutes, but you go with the police. I'll find you wherever you are if you're with them. Just wait at the bus station until they come. Okay?"

"Okay. I'll wait here." *He believed me. Thank you God. You made him believe me.* Silje felt relief, but also fear. Fear of what would happen next. *What if they weren't children after all? What if they were dogs, or other animals? No, they were children. I saw the fingers clutching the bars on one of the cages. Those were real fingers. I heard the crying of one of them before the man shut him up. It was a child. I know it was. It was!*

The police came before Silje expected. The waiting room of the bus station was empty. Two buses had come and gone while Silje was in the ticket office, and she was startled when two uniformed policemen came through the door and walked directly toward her. She stood up from the creaky bench.

"Are you Silje Reiersen?" said one who seemed to be in charge.

"Yes."

"I'm Sergeant Milburn. This is Officer Brower. Come with us please. We'll talk in the car." Silje followed the two men to a couple of police cars double-parked in the street in front of the station. Milburn held the passenger-side door open for her, and she climbed inside. Officer Brower got into a police car parked just behind the first one; someone else was driving that one, Silje noticed with alarm.

What am I doing here? I want to just get on the bus and go home. What if I was wrong? What will they do to me? Ma and Pa don't know where I am. Please, Sheriff Iverson, come and get me. "Do you know Sheriff Joe Iverson in Viroqua?" asked Silje.

"Yes, we've worked a number of cases together. Good man. He will meet us in the alley, but first you have to direct me to where you saw the truck."

"Okay. We have to go south to Third Street and then west," said Silje. "I think I'll recognize the tavern where I turned into the alley."

As they drove the few blocks south, Officer Milburn questioned Silje gently. "Are you from Viroqua?"

"No, Westby. I come to LaCrosse on Saturdays to an optometrist who gives me eye exercises."

"Do you have trouble seeing?" Milburn asked.

"No, not really, but the doctor is going to change my glasses and he wants to strengthen my eyes before he writes the new prescription. I've been coming here on Saturdays since last spring."

Officer Milburn turned onto Third Street. "So you're sure it was children in cages that you saw?"

"Pretty sure. I heard one of them cry out, and I saw fingers on the side of one cage. They moved inside the cages, but they didn't look like animals. It's coming up; the alley is in the next block."

"What were you doing in the alley?"

"I get bored waiting for the bus to leave, so I walk around LaCrosse just looking at things. There. There it is. That's the alley I turned into, and there's another short wide alley that runs between this one and the next alley over."

"Yes, I know the one. It's all warehouses in there." Sergeant Milburn activated his radio and gave instructions to police in other cars to approach the cross-alley from both main alleys leading to it. Milburn slowed the police car as he turned into the cross-alley.

The truck was gone.

"Which door were they loading from?" asked Milburn. Another police car was following them, and two more had just turned into the cross-alley just ahead.

"That one, I think," said Silje. "Yes, it must have been that one." She pointed to a heavy door in a wall set back slightly from the alley. It appeared to be a smaller building than those on either side. *What if I'm wrong? What if I didn't see anything at all? What if I was daydreaming and just believed my thoughts?*

The alley was quiet except for police slamming doors as they got out of their cars. "Stay in the car," Milburn ordered. He opened his door and joined his fellow police officers. Silje watched as one of the policemen tried the door. Locked. Another one pounded on the heavy door yelling, "Police! Open up!" No response.

"Wait," Milburn said. "Quiet. Hear that?" A scream sounded dimly from somewhere inside the warehouse. Then another one.

Through the open window of the police car, Silje heard it too. Distress. Someone was in distress. *Wait. I know that voice. I've heard it before. Where?* Silje searched her mind trying to locate that voice, that sound. Where had she heard screams like that? *Games, that's where. We scream at basketball games and football and even baseball sometimes. I know that voice. I know who it is!*

Silje opened the car door, jumped out, and ran around the other side to where the policemen were milling in front of the door. "I know that voice!" she shouted. "I know who it is! That's Mary Jane. She was taken last spring before school ended. She's from Westby too. She's one of the kidnaped children!"

Milburn glanced her way and then back to the door. "Get the ram. We'll batter the door in," he ordered. Within minutes, the door's old dry wood splintered and fell inward with a crash. Police streamed into the warehouse, guns drawn and spread out in multiple directions. Silje followed at a safe distance hoping that they wouldn't tell her to go back outside. She heard the sound of faint moaning; it must be Mary Jane. She ran to a room on the left and through the partially open door.

"Wait!" yelled a policeman. Silje ignored him. He ran after her.

The room stank of sweat and urine and feces. It was smaller than the huge room filled with metal shelves, scattered cartons and debris. The police officer switched on the lights, and Silje could see filthy pallets strewn about, a pile of children's dirty wet clothing near a large washtub in one corner filled with what looked like old soapy water. Small patches of foam floated on top reflecting vague rainbow colors from the ceiling light.

A slight movement on a pallet caught her eye. She saw it writhe and bend and heard Mary Jane's scream, weaker now. "Mary Jane!" called Silje as she approached her classmate. "Mary Jane, is that you?"

The girl groaned and rolled over. "Who's there? Who are you? They all left. They left me behind." She began to cry. "They just left me here alone." The sobs grew stronger, louder, and uncontrollable.

"In here!" yelled the policeman. As the other police came running in, Silje heard Milburn tell someone to get an ambulance right away.

"Move the vehicles so it can get close to the door. Find out who owns this building and who has been using it. Silje, tell me again what the truck looked like.

"It was big and white, old-looking. . . ."

"Any markings on it?"

"I didn't see any, but I only saw it from the back. It had double doors on the back and it was high. The ramp was steep and the men were having problems swinging some of the cages up. I could hear them swearing when a cage slipped, but they didn't drop any that I saw."

"Did it have a separate cab or was it attached?"

"Attached, I think."

"How long before you called Sheriff Iverson?"

"I don't know, maybe fifteen or twenty minutes, no more. I ran all the way to the bus station and called right away."

"All right." As Milburn walked swiftly away, she heard him say to another policeman, "It can't have gone far. Alert the state troopers: Wisconsin, Illinois, and Minnesota. Large white truck, possibly an old moving van, double doors on back, no discernible markings on sides."

Mary Jane moaned and pulled her knees up and rubbed her abdomen. Silje knelt down beside her. "It's all right, Mary Jane. We've found you. The ambulance is coming to take you to the hospital."

"My name," she said. "What's my name?"

Surprised, Silje answered, "Mary Jane Mason. You're Mary Jane Mason from down near Coon Valley. I know you. We're in the same high school class in Westby. We were in Phys Ed together. Remember?"

"Silje," she moaned. "Stay with me, please. Don't leave me. Don't leave me alone with him please."

Who is 'he?' Who is the 'him' she is talking about? "I won't leave you. I promise. The ambulance will be here soon. Does your stomach hurt?"

Mary Jane nodded. "The baby is trying to come, but it's too early. I'm pregnant."

"I know," said Silje. "Rich told us. He's been frantic to find you."

"Is he all right?"

"Yes, someone found him, and he called the sheriff as soon as he got home. Your parents have been looking for you too. We've all been worried about you." Silje paused, looking down at Mary Jane's pale face and closed eyes. "But you're safe now," she said softly. Soon you'll be home again."

"Say my name, Silje, please," begged Mary Jane.

"Mary Jane. Your name is Mary Jane Mason."

"Again. . . ."

"Mary Jane. Mary Jane Mason from near Coon Valley. You're going to marry Rich Dahlen. He loves you, and you'll see him soon." Silje reached for Mary Jane's hand and held it in both of hers as she watched the dozing girl. She heard sirens outside, faint at first, then loud as the ambulance came up the alley. The sirens stopped abruptly, and in moments, the ambulance crew entered the warehouse and came into the room in which Mary Jane lay. Silje rose to her feet as the crew approached.

"Silje! Stay with me. Please!" pleaded Mary Jane, her eyes wide with fear. "Don't let him take me. . . ."

"It's just the ambulance, Mary Jane. They're driving you to the hospital. You'll be safe there."

Sheriff Iverson appeared at Silje's side. "Are you okay?" he asked.

"Yes," she answered, "but I think one of the men loading children saw me before I ran. He knows what I look like."

"Don't worry. He doesn't know who you are, and he's not going to find out. I'll see to that."

Mary Jane was on the gurney being wheeled out. "Silje!" she called.

"Can I go with her? She's so scared," asked Silje.

"Come on. I'll go out to the ambulance with you. We'll see if there's enough room for you to ride inside with her."

Just before Silje climbed into the ambulance, she said, "What about my parents? I'll be late coming home. I missed the four o'clock bus, so I have to be on the eight o'clock bus for sure."

"I'll call them and let them know you'll be coming back later this evening with me. I have to leave you now. I've got some things to work out with the LaCrosse police." He paused. "This is going to get complicated," he muttered. "Listen Silje, you've done a good thing here, a great job. I'm going to call the Masons and the Dahlens and let them know that we've found Mary Jane. You wait at Lutheran General until I come to get you." The sheriff was gone as suddenly as he had arrived.

The ride to the hospital took no time at all. Then it was a whirlwind of emergency room exams, waiting, more exams, and finally being assigned to a room on the obstetrics ward. Mary Jane seemed confused about who she was, so Silje gave an official-looking woman the girl's name, address, and age; Mary Jane's parents would have to fill in the rest.

What on earth has happened to her? How could she forget who she was in just a few months? Mary Jane and I, we are classmates, but really, we barely know each other, yet she's clinging to me as if I'm her last best hope, her lifeline to sanity. God, what did they do to her? Are all the other lost children the same way?

Silje sat by the window in Mary Jane's hospital room watching doctors and nurses come and go. A bottle hung upside down from a stand, and a long tube led from the bottom of the bottle to a needle that had been pushed into the top of Mary Jane's hand while they were still in the emergency room. A nurse came and injected a medication of some sort into a rubber connector on the top of the tubing where the liquid dripped slowly and continuously into a small glass drip container. The nurse watched the drip, made some adjustments and left the room. She didn't speak to Mary Jane or to Silje. Mary Jane dozed fitfully, occasionally calling out so softly that Silje could barely hear her, "Say my name. Say it again."

Silje had heard a doctor say that the contractions had stabilized, and the patient wouldn't lose the baby. The room quieted down, so Silje moved her chair close to the bed and took Mary Jane's hand in hers. "You're all right now, Mary Jane. The baby is safe. You're safe."

"They left me behind because they thought I was too sick to go on the truck," she whispered, opening her eyes. I had terrible cramps, and I couldn't stop screaming no matter how much they slapped me and told me to shut up. It hurt so much."

"The baby saved you then," said Silje. "You're going to have Rich's baby, and that's what saved you. The baby is how we found you. He, or maybe it's a she, was making you call out so that the police would break down the door and we could find you."

"Yes . . . ," she whispered. "My baby."

"So this little baby is a miracle baby. We can be so glad that you are pregnant. You can thank God every day for what this baby did for you."

Before Mary Jane drifted off again, Silje felt she had to ask her, "Did you see Clara Mitby in the warehouse? Remember the girl who disappeared when we were sophomores?"

"I don't know. I remember when she was taken, but I'd never known her. Nobody was called Clara, but he changed everybody's name, and we weren't allowed to say our own name anymore. He called me. . . ." The sedative took hold, and she probably wouldn't wake up for a while. Silje let go of Mary Jane's hand and stood up. She stretched and walked to the window. It was growing dark, but still light enough to see the parking lot.

I wonder where the other children are. There were so many of them being loaded into that truck. They must feel cramped and uncomfortable, especially the ones doubled up, two to a cage. Maybe some had three to a cage, I don't know, I didn't see that.

That man that chased me. If he had caught me, would he have put me into a cage too? I can't think about that. Sheriff Iverson said that those men would never find out that it was me that saw them. He must think that I might be in danger if they know. She shuddered.

A commotion in the hall caught her attention. A moment later, an older couple entered the room and went to the sleeping girl on the bed. The woman, probably Mary Jane's mother, was crying, and the older man put his arm around her. Close behind, came another couple following Rich Dahlen. Rich quickly came to the other side of the bed, sat down in the chair that Silje had occupied and took Mary Jane's hand. "Thank God. Thank God," he said softly. "I thought I'd lost you."

Mary Jane drifted out of sleep and saw Rich. She smiled. "I thought I'd lost you too," she whispered. "Here, feel this." She took Rich's hand and moved it over the sheet to her swelling abdomen. "Our baby," she said.

Silje crept around the edges of the crowd in the room and went out into the hallway. Her job was done. One of the missing children had been found and would soon be home. *Where were the rest? Would the police find the truck and all the children in it? Would they be able to stop it? Would Clara be on that truck, even though Mary Jane hadn't seen her? Please God, let them find Clara. She needs to come home too. I'll help her find her parents wherever they are now. I will. I promise.*

The tiny waiting room at the entrance to the obstetrics ward was empty. Silje put a quarter in the drinks machine and caught the can of cola rolling out below. She turned the pages of a magazine as she sipped her drink, but couldn't concentrate. Too much had happened. She was tired and wanted to go home. She didn't have to wait long. Only a few minutes had passed when Sheriff Iverson found her there. "Ready to go?" he asked. Silje nodded and followed him out.

They didn't talk much on the ride back to Westby. Sheriff Iverson told her that the Illinois State Troopers had spotted the truck just over the line into Illinois heading toward Chicago. "That means that the FBI will get involved. Maybe we can break up this child trafficking once and for all."

"I hope so," said Silje. "Did they get the children back?"

"Last information I had was that the Illinois State Troopers were calling for local school buses to help bring the kids back to LaCrosse."

"Where will they stay?"

"I think they've arranged for them to be taken to the gym at a high school near Lutheran General. There were so many of them, almost two hundred, I'm told. Then they'll be examined and interviewed at the hospital, one by one, and released to their parents. There were kids from all over Wisconsin and Minnesota too. It's a big operation How many men did you see loading the truck?"

"There were two up in the back of the truck and maybe four or five on the ground bringing the cages out on dollies. It seemed like one was the boss giving orders to the rest."

"Think you'd recognize any of them?"

"I don't think so. They were too far away and mostly had their backs to me. No, I don't think so. Anyway, I was looking at the cages."

"When the truck was stopped, there was only the driver and one other man," mused the sheriff. "So the rest must be from LaCrosse, or locally at least."

They rode in silence for a while until Silje asked, "Was that where Archie would have been if he wouldn't have escaped?"

"Not sure. We haven't connected Myron Larson to the people he was working with. All he ever had was a phone number to call and the meeting place was never the same. If we catch more members of the LaCrosse ring, and Larson can identify one of them as his contact, then we'll know."

"What about the phone number?"

"We're still tracing it. We'll find it, but by the time we do, the contact may be long gone, especially if he knows we've got Larson."

"It's been in the newspaper that his trial is coming up."

"Exactly."

The Vernon County police car swung off Highway 27 and over the tracks into the driveway of the Reiersen farm. "I'll walk you to the door, but I can't come in. I've gotta stop at the office before I head home."

Alex and Pauline came out on the porch as Silje and the sheriff got out of the car and walked toward the house followed by the dog who had barked only once when the car came to a stop. Pal knew this car, and that it was accepted by the family.

"Listen Silje. It would be safer if you didn't mention to anyone that you were the one who discovered and reported the truck loading the children. The LaCrosse police agreed to keep your name out of it, and Otto Bakke will be the only one that I will tell. It won't be written in any records."

"Should I tell Ma and Pa?"

"Yes, but warn them not to say anything about it to anyone else. We don't know who these people are, and we know that others are still at large."

Sheriff Iverson greeted Alex and Pauline, saying, "You've got a brave daughter here. She'll tell you why she was late. I'd like to stay and talk awhile, but I have to run. I'll stop by in a couple of days. Goodnight Silje."

“Goodnight,” she answered turning and pushing her way past her parents. “I’m hungry,” said Silje as she entered the kitchen. “Is there anything to eat?”

21

Guidelines for Life

Silje never saw Mary Jane again. Later that fall, after school had begun, she heard Edwin tell someone that Mary Jane and Rich had a baby boy and that they were married and living with her parents. Silje didn't ask Edwin for details.

The news of the child trafficking ring spread like wildfire throughout the states involved, front page headlines filling most newspapers for weeks. Myron Larson's trial was covered day-by-day. Viroqua had never seen so many journalists and photographers; the motels and hotels were filled for miles around for the four-day trial, and as suddenly as it had begun, it was over. Vernon County settled back into a routine of sorts. Harvesting had continued throughout the hoopla, of course, but talk of the kidnaper from Sparta arose in almost every conversation for weeks after the trial and sentencing were over.

Larson was convicted of Archie's kidnaping and sentenced to sixty years in prison with no parole. It was thought that he may have been involved in at least eight more kidnapings over the years, so the investigation was ongoing. His contact had not yet been found.

It's funny how friendships change. I see Alice in the hallway between classes sometimes, but we don't hang out anymore. Caroline has gotten a bit too wild for my taste. We're all still friends, I guess, but since neither of them ride the Coon Valley school bus, getting together just doesn't happen anymore.

Thank goodness for Tillie. Since she started going out with my cousin Merlin, I at least get to go places. They invite me to go everywhere with them, and usually we pick up other kids so that it's a group.

Carl Nelson just got back from Korea, and he likes me. He's not very tall, and definitely not good-looking, but he's a friend of Merlin's and lives on Highway 27, so he comes with us often. He's fun, and I like him. The big brown scab on his chin seems to be healing, so maybe we'll kiss when it's gone. Who knows? He says it started growing in Korea, but he doesn't know what it's from.

Silje was quiet at home, and did whatever she was asked to do. She hadn't told Alex and Pauline much about what happened in LaCrosse that day, only that she saw a lot of police cars and that's what caused her to miss the bus.

"So why did Sheriff Iverson tell us that you were so brave?" asked Pauline.

"Oh, just because I was able to point out where the truck had been and then they found Mary Jane," answered Silje nonchalantly.

Pauline looked at her quizzically, but asked no more questions. Her daughter had always been a puzzle to her, often withdrawn and seemingly not present even when she was right there in front of her. The sheriff had stopped by the farm and mentioned that while the investigation was going on, it would be better if Alex and Pauline said nothing about Silje being in La-Crosse that day.

Silje was a high school senior now, and felt that she was much more mature than last year. She paid better attention in class, did all her homework well and on time. Her grades went up in all her classes.

I need good grades if I'm going to college next year. Ma and Pa said I could go. They didn't like the idea of me going to art school in Milwaukee like I really wanted to; it was too risky, they said, too full of people living in sin. And they said "no way" to the idea of me joining the Air Force with Alice. We would have done it together; that should have been safe enough. So college was the only thing left.

If I want to leave Westby, I have to find a way where Ma and Pa can help me for a while. I wouldn't know how to do it on my own. Only a couple of my cousins on Pa's side that I know of have ever gone to college so far. Nobody on Ma's side; I'd be the first. Maybe that's why she's so anxious for me to go. She'd be more important around here in the family. She seems important enough to my way of thinking. Everyone comes to her for advice and help.

As much as she wanted to leave all with which she was familiar, the thought of leaving frightened her. What if she couldn't understand the subjects in college? What if they were too hard? What if she flunked something?

Yeah and what if I died in a car crash too? C'mon Silje. Get your act together. All the mind tricks have been under control for some time except that pesky bubble that still comes sometimes, and I still hate spiders although I don't go into a total panic like I used to, well mostly I don't.

I can do this. I can. If I work hard this year and keep getting good grades, they'll let me into college. They will. If I think of all the great things I've learned in life, if I keep them always in mind, I'll be able to survive out there. Let's see:

-Don't get trapped where you can't get out of whatever you've gotten yourself into.

-Never put your feelings into writing. You never know who might see it.

-Run faster than you ever thought you could and don't look backwards when being chased.

-Be careful all the time, because the world is not a safe place.

-Try to find something good even in bad things. It makes you feel better.

-Rely on yourself, because that's mostly all you've got, except for God, of course. He will give me the strength that I need to carry on.

Thank you God.

Glossary for the 1950s

Burning grass: A subspecies of stinging nettles found throughout North America causing painful raised pustules on the skin upon contact.

Dork: Slang for a stupid or inept person.

Duck Tail: A heavily greased style of hair worn by young men who considered themselves nonconformist. Similar to that worn later by Elvis Presley.

Greyhound: The bus company providing transportation and package delivery among small towns throughout North America.

Home room: The school room to where high school students went when not assigned to a class.

Oilcloth: Close-woven cotton or linen fabric treated with a coating of linseed oil to make it waterproof.

Omncient: Knowing everything.

Omnipotent: Having unlimited power.

Palmer Method: A system of cursive writing and practice whereby elementary school students were taught penmanship.

Penny Loafers: A type of slip-on shoe where a penny can be inserted into a slit on the top of the shoe.

REA: The Rural Electrification Administration of the U.S. Department of Agriculture that provided loans to rural organizations to bring electricity to farms.

About the Author

R.Z. Halleson wrote *God's Child: Unraveling* at age 77 as a part of a series of stand-alone novels exploring the theme of good and evil and the role that "God" plays in a world that struggles to understand itself.

"I'd like to live to be a hundred," she says. "There are so many stories to tell and so much more to be learned about our complicated selves and relationships.

Acknowledgements

I would like to thank Commander Terry Shiel of the Skokie, Illinois police department for reviewing parts of the manuscript. I am grateful also to his son Peter Shiel for his amazing patience.

24916895R00165

Made in the USA
Charleston, SC
11 December 2013